"Let me show you the stars," Adam said.

"I don't usually enter dark bedrooms with men after knowing them all of eight hours." Maggie tried to chuckle, but her heart was rocketing so hard, she swore it echoed off the walls.

"It's the view I want you to see." He pushed up the shade.

"Adam, it's magnificent," she murmured. Stars glittered through the heavens—bright, blinding, and breath-stealing.

Then Maggie turned around to look at Adam. They were alone. In his bedroom. "I feel a little light-headed. Do you think that's from the weightlessness?"

"Could be. The heart pounds in funny ways up here." He touched the pulse on the side of her neck. "Mind if I show you?"

There was something extremely erotic about giving someone permission to touch you, Maggie thought.

"Consider it a scientific experiment," he said gently, sensing her self-consciousness. He reached in under her long hair and touched her skin.

Lack of gravity wasn't the only thing making her float. Inside, everything turned liquid; flares shot up like sunspots when he ran his fingertips down her throat.

"I never imagined so many stars," she said, catching their reflection in his eyes.

"Have you ever imagined this?" he asked, and brushed her lips with his. . . .

WHAT ARE *LOVESWEPT* ROMANCES?

They are stories of true romance and touching emotion. We believe those two very important ingredients are constants in our highly sensual and very believable stories in the *LOVESWEPT* line. Our goal is to give you, the reader, stories of consistently high quality that may sometimes make you laugh, sometimes make you cry, but are always fresh and creative and contain many delightful surprises within their pages.

Most romance fans read an enormous number of books. Those they truly love, they keep. Others may be traded with friends and soon forgotten. We hope that each *LOVESWEPT* romance will be a treasure—a "keeper." We will always try to publish

LOVE STORIES YOU'LL NEVER FORGET
BY AUTHORS YOU'LL ALWAYS REMEMBER

The Editors

Loveswept ®517

Terry Lawrence
Ever Since Adam

BANTAM BOOKS
NEW YORK · TORONTO · LONDON · SYDNEY · AUCKLAND

EVER SINCE ADAM

A Bantam Book / January 1992

If you would be interested in receiving protective vinyl
covers for your Loveswept books, please write to this
address for information:

Loveswept
Bantam Books
P.O. Box 985
Hicksville, NY 11802

ISBN 0-553-44187-6

Published simultaneously in the United States and Canada

Bantam Books are published by Bantam Books, a division
of Bantam Doubleday Dell Publishing Group, Inc. Its trade-
mark, consisting of the words "Bantam Books" and the
portrayal of a rooster, is Registered in U.S. Patent and Trade-
mark Office and in other countries. Marca Registrada.
Bantam Books, 666 Fifth Avenue, New York, New York 10103.

PRINTED IN THE UNITED STATES OF AMERICA

OPM   0 9 8 7 6 5 4 3 2 1

One

The first time Maggie saw Adam Strade, he was twenty feet high, a face on the big screen in Houston, NASA's rising star transmitting from orbit.

He'd winked at her.

Yes, her, Maggie had told herself after an instinctive rush to deny it. Twenty-foot winks were hard to ignore.

She'd consoled herself with the knowledge that his own monitor on Space Station McAuliffe had a twelve-inch screen. She'd seen a giant of space exploration; he'd seen a fuzzy, nine-inch woman.

And yet an unidentifiable effervescence had hovered over her for days. She'd tried to dismiss the feeling but hadn't succeeded—until Hal Dane, director of Mission Control, had assigned her to six weeks in space with Adam Strade.

The opportunity to spend six weeks doing on-site research! Six weeks experiencing life in the quarters she'd helped design thrilled her—and overshadowed any unnerving thoughts about being alone with Adam.

Careerwise it was too good to be true. There had to be a catch, she thought.

There was.

• • •

"I'm Margaret Mead Mullins, novice astronaut."

Maggie tucked her helmet under her arm and extended her gloved hand, very aware the bulky space suit made her look like an orange Michelin tire man. Her first goal was to make a good impression on Commander Strade. "Wonderful to meet you, sir."

"Miss Mullins," Adam replied, neatly avoiding the glove and going straight to the metal closing ring at her wrist. "Let me undo this for you. We'll do it right."

From what she'd heard, doing things right was a credo with Strade. He was a man of strict standards, possessed of a tough personal code few men mastered. His own goal was to head the three-year mission to Mars now on the drawing board at NASA.

Her mission was to make his life and that of his future crews easier, more efficient, and as comfortable as possible. At least, that had been the original plan until Hal had taken her aside just before lift-off.

The sensation of skin on skin startled her out of her reverie. With a few deft movements Adam had uncoupled the glove from her sleeve and clasped her bare hand in a firm handshake. She bobbed slightly in the zero-gravity atmosphere of the welcoming bay along with her three fellow astronauts.

"You're in charge here," she noted, hoping to commence with light conversation.

"Innkeeper to the stars." An expansive man might have waved a hand toward the interior with a proprietary air. Adam Strade simply flicked his wrist, then got to the point. "You're our visiting psychologist."

Maggie blinked. Apparently nothing got by Adam Strade. Did Hal think *she* would? "I'm an ergonomics specialist, actually, here to observe living conditions and how crews adapt to them. We want to make daily life as comfortable and as conducive to productivity as possible."

"Is that all?" There was a shrewdness in his expression.

She managed a shrug. "Wouldn't want anyone getting claustrophobic way up here." Maggie tacked on a smile, keeping a sigh of relief strictly to herself as he turned toward the others. So much for first impressions.

And her impressions? A quick word association brought "cowboy," "bronco buster," "pirate," and "all-American hero" to mind. Each term already a part of the space-age derring-do of the Adam Strade myth.

Not very original, she thought.

She attempted to see beyond the myth, and immediately noticed a tension that stood out on him like a porcupine's quills.

Was it because of her psychology background? Or because she'd hidden the truth? she wondered.

It wasn't her fault Hal had pulled her aside hours before lift-off. "We'd appreciate it if you'd use that psychology background of yours to check him out, see how he's holding up," he'd said.

"I have a degree, but that doesn't mean I've practiced—"

"So you're less than a pro but more than an amateur. You two really hit it off that time you relayed data for us."

Before she'd jumped in with a carefully formed excuse for that wink, Hal had gotten to the real reason. "It doesn't take a psychologist to form an opinion. In six weeks you two will have plenty of time to get to know each other."

But how well? Maggie thought, her resolve quailing now that she'd seen Adam up close. And he'd seen her. Did he suspect the real reason Hal had sent her? Her ideas on capsule design were all very fine, but the director wanted a personal assessment of the mental and emotional state of Adam Strade. Maggie had to get close enough to find out, porcupine quills and all.

Conferring with the three astronauts who had accompanied her on the shuttle, Adam glanced her way. Maggie colored and fumbled with her suit.

Strade was a quick judge of people—and a good one. According to his record, he was self-reliant, unpretentious, and always aware of his duty. He'd been a test pilot and a popular instructor at the academy.

And yet there'd been rumors, hints, disquiet. A fearless jet jockey had become a loner—not overnight, and not in any way people could put a finger on. Everyone in Houston had a theory. No one had an answer. Maggie had been handed the unenviable job of producing one.

She realized she could barely come up with a description of the man she'd known a scant five minutes. Maggie made some mental notes: His lashes were dark brown, his hair the color of an old leather bomber jacket. He wore it long on top, short and severe on the sides—military and maverick both.

His skin was bronzed and crinkled. The scientist in her recognized the results of weekly sunlamp sessions to assist in the absorption of vitamin D. The woman in her said it worked—on a number of levels. The muscles revealed by his short-sleeved shirt indicated he used the resistance exercises NASA had designed for the space program. He was disciplined about his body.

Less visible was the air of competence that allowed him to run this space station single-handedly—no help requested or required. *Time* magazine had once called him the bravest man in the galaxy. Maybe the loneliest, Maggie thought, letting the insight sink in.

"How's it feel?" he asked, moving smoothly across the room to her.

Her legs shook, her cheeks flushed, and her pulse commenced a series of little dips. "Exciting," she answered honestly. "Docking with a fully functional orbiting space station is quite a feat."

"Quite." He studied her again with those shrewd eyes.

"Quite a setup." She nodded at the spanking white walls with their banks of blinking lights and braided cables.

"You don't look impressed, Ms. Mullins."

"Maggie, please."

"Then call me Adam."

He shook her hand again. His was large and warm, and in this completely calculated environment reassuringly human. Maggie wanted to cling to it for a moment.

She indicated the room instead. "Considering the miracle of space travel, they could've made this more appealing. The accordion entry from the shuttle to the station looks like a back entrance to O'Hare."

"You wanted rows of purple plastic chairs?" His eyes twinkled when he teased, although the rest of his face remained carefully neutral. He wasn't the only one being sized up. "Maybe a luggage carousel?"

"How about piped-in music?" she retorted, playing along. "Or flight attendants?"

"Now *that* I wouldn't mind. Maybe I'll requisition one next time."

Maggie's fellow astronauts joined in the laughter.

Dr. H. E. Grigg, a NASA scientist, was on his second mission in space, following up experiments he'd put in place on his first journey. Joe Fontaine, a specialist in molecular dynamics from the University of Chicago, had been chosen to perform further intricate experiments in his field. Major Wells was on a military mission, highly secret and therefore reported in all the newspapers as the realignment of a spy satellite over the Middle East.

"I'm sorry it wasn't a better reception." Adam's voice grated like fine gravel.

Not used often enough, Maggie thought, the specter of loneliness drifting by like a soft breeze. "I know

I sound like a hard-to-please tourist, but this has all the charm of a Radio Shack warehouse."

"A billion-dollar one. Every one of these cables is essential. Every inch of this place is designed to be practical and functional."

And comfortable? A man needed that too. At least Maggie could provide him with that.

"It gets better inside." He tilted his head toward a short passageway leading to a hatchway and a ladder, and the main station. "How was takeoff?"

The question was intended for anyone who cared to answer. Dr. Grigg gave the most technically accurate response, Major Wells offered the briefest, and Joe Fontaine repeated what the radio operator had told them as they'd cleared the atmosphere. When her turn came, all Maggie remembered was trying very hard to keep her breakfast down.

"Maggie? How was it for you?"

She wasn't quite sure she liked the way he'd phrased that. "Blast-off was amazing." She caught his wince; not the first time she'd failed to answer that question to a man's satisfaction. "Am I sounding like a tourist again?"

She waved the glove clutched in her hand. She wanted to set it down somewhere, but it wouldn't stay put. It drifted to nose level every time she let it go, hovering like a floating crab inches from her face.

"It's quite an experience," he countered mildly, taking the troublesome glove, "even when you've been up as many times as I have. It isn't easy to forget you're sitting on thousands of tons of rocket fuel while they count down to ignition."

Her smile thanked him for understanding, and she took a deep breath. "Every nerve in my body was on end. When we actually lifted off, the G-forces were like having a dozen mattresses pressed to my chest. You know that story *The Princess and the Pea*? I felt like the pea."

He laughed, a deeper, rougher sound. My, she liked that.

"How do you feel now?"

Maggie took stock of her body first; her emotions were bouncing around like beams off a satellite. "This floating is strange."

"Zero gravity."

The man could make anything sound sexy. Too bad she couldn't ask what effects this sensation had on a person's libido—there had to be a correlation. She'd never reacted this palpably to a man. The kid sister, the pal, that was Maggie.

Meanwhile Dr. Grigg had calmly shed his own suit, revealing the plain shirt and jogging pants that would be his on-board uniform. Major Wells got to work helping Joe Fontaine. Adam removed Maggie's suit. Her temperature rose one degree with every buckle.

The suit, airtight, lightweight, wired with communication equipment and an atmosphere pack, came in connecting pieces. The legs, arms, and torso disconnected—provided trembling fingers remembered how. Struggling with the zipper under her arm, Adam pulled her feet right off the ground.

But there was no ground, Maggie realized. Up and down were relative concepts there. Despite that fact the station was designed to orient its inhabitants in one direction. Somehow, one didn't mind floating sideways if one saw where one was in relation to everything else.

In other words, a person liked to know which way was up.

Unbuckling another clamp, Adam gave her a nudge, and she revolved toward the ceiling, slipping out of her pants and boots as she did so.

"Whoa!" She held on to a rope of colored cables and pushed herself away from the ceiling with more effort than strictly required, bumping back to the floor with a thump. "Oh my Lord." Overcorrecting that, she bounced straight against Adam's chest.

Her hand splayed on his navy polo shirt, specifically the NASA insignia sewn over his left nipple. She felt a distinct nub under her palm. Whether it was due to the jostling or her touch, Maggie didn't dare ask.

Tentatively, she pushed off, twirling easily in one direction, watching in dismay as he was nudged in the other. "Opposite and equal reactions," she muttered.

"Don't worry, happens all the time."

It wasn't physical; it was physics. That didn't stop Maggie from wondering for a split second if his reaction could in any way be equal to hers. "I'm sure I'll get used to this in a minute."

"Space orientation's easy when you get the hang of it."

Easier than understanding beautiful women, Adam thought. He could have bet a moment ago the color in her cheeks was a reaction to his touch, that when her eyes widened in wonder, it was because a spark of awareness glimmered there.

Why not? He was incredibly aware of her. It was a treat unveiling the body inside that suit.

Of course, he could be wrong about her response. Wouldn't be the first time where women were concerned. A familiar ache constricted his chest.

Maybe it was hormones. Maybe he'd been in space too damn long. Maybe the oxygen mix was acting up again. He made a mental note to check, wondering if the air pressure had any relation to the imprint of her hand lingering on his chest or the reedy trace of perfume drifting by.

The thought rankled him: If Hal *had* to send a shrink, why not a Grigg clone? The director of Mission Control had personally assigned Adam sixteen months on this space station to welcome crews and to man it alone between missions. But ever since

Adam had volunteered for Mars, Hal had been asking questions, waxing eloquent on the value of hearth and home.

Adam wanted none of it. Seeking solitude, some men chose a basement workshop, a hunting cabin, a stint in the Foreign Legion. It just so happened Adam craved space. Outer space.

But did Hal listen? No. No sooner had Adam put a halt to his waxy eloquence than Maggie Mullins had promptly been awarded six weeks on a space station most scientists couldn't get six days on. To do what, study comfort zones? Determine if thirty by ninety inches was room enough in which to sling a hammock?

Balderdash. Hal didn't think Adam was losing it; Hal thought he was blind, deaf, and dumber than moon rocks. The biodata on the computer said Ms. Mullins had a shrink background. Shrink she was.

The woman floated by again, about to bump her head of curly red hair into a panel of sensors. Adam caught one of her gray-socked feet and tugged her back. "You want to be down here or up there?"

"Here is fine." She intently examined every part of the welcoming bay except his face.

Adam ducked his head and got her to look at him, seeking the color of her eyes. Hazel-brown with green flecks and a gold corona. That was nice to know.

She was no doubt wired from the trip. Some man-to-woman attention might settle her down, bring her back to earth, so to speak.

"You okay?" he asked softly. He tacked on the sexy growl for her benefit only. "I know this is your first time."

She blushed a pretty pink under a galaxy of freckles he hadn't noticed before.

Obviously, he was sorely out of practice with this charm business. He'd wanted to make her feel at ease; that was his job. How'd he know she'd react like that? "I meant, how's it going?" he asked.

"When I'm not banging into things?" Maggie felt totally off balance and blamed it on his arms.

"You're decompressing. Novices need to experience it. Go ahead, play with it." He gave her a mild shove in the right direction.

She responded to his dare and wound backward around the bay. "This feels so . . . so silly."

"And?"

"Weightless. Emotionally as well as physically. Kind of carefree." She did a layout three-sixty she remembered from diving class and laughed out loud. It probably wasn't the most dignified introduction to space, or Adam Strade, but it was useless to pretend it wasn't fun. "You know, play is a form of practice. Maybe all newcomers should do this so they get used to maneuvering up here."

"I think they do," Adam replied. "I've caught more than one guest doing somersaults on the sly. Like it?"

As if she were swimming through silky water, she propelled herself across the ceiling with a tiny kick. A trace of her Georgia childhood crept into her speech. "It's more fun than doing a cannonball into a still pond on a hot day."

"As we say where I come from, it's more fun than an F-23 in a tumble at thirty thousand feet."

"Oh." For some reason the tumbling idea made her stomach follow suit. Picturing this man purposely putting a jet through the most rigorous stress tests, hurtling toward the ground at speeds approaching—

She gulped and touched the ceiling, pushing herself back to the floor. Closing her eyes, she took a few deep breaths.

Adam's voice rumbled at the other end of the room. "How are you doing, Joe?"

Joe Fontaine went pale, patches of unmistakable gray dotting his cheeks. He held as closely to the wall as possible, rigorously adhering to his idea of up. Space sickness, a version of motion sickness, was taking its toll.

No wonder he hadn't joined Maggie on her jaunt around the welcoming bay.

"It's interesting," Joe said, lips compressed in a tight smile. "The takeoff, all of it. Very interesting."

"Don't gush too much," Adam teased gruffly.

Major Wells gave a blunt laugh. "Vomit and get it over with," he ordered brusquely. "That's what I always do."

Joe looked as if he might take Wells up on the idea right there.

"Why don't you show him the living quarters, Major?" Adam suggested.

"Sure thing, Commander. Come on, son."

"Nice to see you again, Adam," Dr. Grigg said, following the others up the hatchway to mid-deck. Everything was business as usual with him. They might have been meeting outside an elevator in a research facility. "How are my experiments coming?"

"Been watching over 'em as if they were newborn chicks. I followed every instruction and logged each one in. Oh, and Doc?"

Grigg hovered at the hatch opening.

"One of those little suckers has grown a third eye. I think you better have a look at him."

Grigg grunted and closed the hatch behind him.

"Third eye?" Maggie barely kept the squeak out of her voice.

"Experimental mice. He's studying bone loss in space."

"But you said—"

"Kidding." He lifted her chin between his thumb and forefinger. "You're not really going to get sick, are you?"

"Only if those mice are running around loose." She couldn't say for sure, but the jumpiness in her pulse switched to a different beat when he touched her.

She felt less light-headed and at the same time more fluttery. Another observation for her journal.

"They're in cages," Adam reassured her. "Groucho, Chico, Harpo, and Fernando."

"Fernando?"

"Valenzuela. I couldn't remember the other Marx brother's name."

"Zeppo."

Adam snapped his fingers and gave her a grin. "Zeppo Marx. I owe you one. Let me get you out of this." He tugged on her torso unit once more. "Come here, you." Reeling her in as she inadvertently pushed off, he softly commanded her to hold on to his shirt or his belt.

But there was no belt, only a very taut waistline—and a man's hands skillfully and adeptly undressing her.

She firmly reminded herself she wore a complete outfit under her suit. There was no reason to get giddy over a simple touch. When he accidentally, glancingly, skimmed her breast through her shirt, his hand never strayed near it again.

And his eyes never quite met hers.

That's when it occurred to her. If she hadn't been so off balance, she'd have noticed it right away. He was setting limits. Joking. Teasing. Openly admitting an awareness of her as a woman but no more. Exactly the kind of up-front attitude men and women needed when sharing living quarters.

And the only way she could thank him for it was by playing along. *With a little more poise this time, Margaret.*

He stored the torso section with the other pieces of the suit.

"Thank you," Maggie said, "I was beginning to feel like part of the Thanksgiving Day parade. Just tie a rope to me and haul me along."

He chuckled.

"You look so normal," she said, "in comparison, I mean."

In addition to the navy polo shirt and navy cotton pants, he wore soft slippers and a watch with more dials than the dashboard of a Trans Am. For her part, she was glad she'd chosen the aqua outfit—loose slacks and a matching turtleneck. From somewhere in her duffel bag she dredged up a white knit sweater, put it on, and buttoned it up. "They told me it gets chilly up here."

"We keep it at a steady sixty-eight." He eyed her sweater as if a heavy cardigan with pink popcorn stitching were incomparably alluring. Then he gave her a wink. "Nice."

And sweet. And proper enough for parochial school. Maggie moaned inwardly. "My gran made it. She obviously pictured me at the mercy of daredevil space raiders."

"And she wanted you to be warm when they abducted you to their planet?" Shaking his head slowly, Adam lifted her duffel and indicated the way to the main station. "Can't wait to see the flannel nightgown."

His grainy chuckle wafted behind them.

"As the only female guest, you'll have private quarters," Adam stated, sliding open a door to a bedroom and a bath. "Your grandmother's wishes were taken into account."

Maggie laughed, glancing at the sleeping bag slung hammock-style over the desk. For a moment she wondered how one climbed into it, then remembered climbing was hardly necessary.

A lighted mirror came on at the touch of a switch, illuminating the sink. Everything was stowed in built-in drawers. Toothbrush, hairbrush, and comb clicked into little compartments so they wouldn't float around.

Half the drawers had been emptied. "But this is

your room, Commander. I'd hate to displace you."
Maggie turned, trying not to bump into him.

"Like I said, you're our only female guest."

"That isn't exactly the rule."

"I know, we're supposed to be colleagues. No special
privileges, no sexist language. However, command,
as I understand it, means daily operating procedure
is up to me. The lady gets the room."

"You're sure I'm not upsetting your routine?"

"Isn't that what you're here for?"

The smile stuck to her face long after he'd left to see
to the others. He was convinced she was there to
psychoanalyze him and, thanks to Hal's request, she
couldn't categorically deny it. "Caught between Hal's
rock and Adam's hard place," she mused, blinking
away the wildly inappropriate pictures her mind
conjured up.

Alone for the first time in hours, she tried to settle
down. Or up. Or sideways. This floating business got
tiresome after a while. She unzipped the duffel,
catching at items as they drifted up into the room.
Her journal wavered lazily by. She seized it, found a
mechanical pencil in the desk drawer, and jotted
down her immediate impressions, starting with the
physical ones.

Re weightlessness. The heart, used to pumping
blood from the bottom to the top, doesn't know
which way to pump. I feel thick-headed, light on
my feet, and always off balance. Have met Adam
Strade. Any connection?

She firmly penciled a smiley-face in the margin.
She searched the drawer for an eraser.

In a moment she realized she was looking for more
than that. Curiosity warred with professionalism;
she was there to study the living space, not the man.
Strade knew that. Briefed on each guest's mission,

ordered to assist in any way he could, he'd started by putting her in his room.

"Undressing me and putting me in his room," she amended, wondering how that would look on paper.

The man was being cooperative. Flexible. Polite. Attentive to a woman's needs. He had to expect her to examine how he adapted to his living quarters, she theorized. That was her job—and all the rationalization she needed to open the first cupboard.

Everything in it was shipshape. Shirts piled on shirts gently hovering one atop the other. "Bet that cuts down on wrinkles." She grinned.

He'd improvised a catchall for dirty clothes. "Signs of interacting with his environment," she penned.

The underwear drawer was another matter altogether. She might be freely curious, but the sight of his briefs had her slamming the drawer so hard, she bounded back to the hammock again. She didn't want to imagine what he wore under those loose-fitting slacks any more than she wanted to picture those black briefs next to his skin.

She wedged her feet on the floor and her back against the wall, jotting doggedly in her notebook. *He runs a tight but comfortable ship.* Tight. Comfortable. Like his briefs.

"Fiddlesticks," she muttered.

Opening the medicine cabinet to unpack her toiletries, the peppermint scent of his mouthwash gently unfolded into the room. A surprisingly intense memory of his breath feathering her face as he'd struggled with a balky latch on her suit assailed her. *Maggie, How was it for you?*

She caught herself staring into space, then laughed out loud when she realized that's exactly where she was.

She printed furiously. *Men and women in close quarters. Of course a little adult teasing is in order. Obviously that would be of the sexual variety.*

There. It made more sense in black and white as she hovered over Adam Strade's desk, avoiding Adam Strade's toilet articles, studiously forgoing another peek in Adam Strade's underwear drawer.

Maggie? her conscience said.

"Yes, ma'am?"

You're here to study the ship, not the man. You are not here to get in his drawers.

"Yes, ma'am."

Examine your own reactions to living in space. Your own emotions.

Shouldn't be hard. Maggie could quantify, qualify, graph, and plot practically every emotion she'd ever had. Just plain experiencing them was where she fell down.

"Hey, you can't fall when there's no gravity," she said aloud.

The perky smile faded as she glanced at herself in the mirror. Around a narrow face someone once charitably described as foxy, her red hair curled into ringlets. She couldn't blame it on the humidity. The place was air-conditioned and oxygen enriched. The entire atmosphere was completely controlled.

Except for her reactions to Adam Strade, which were anything but.

Two

"I could swear I've heated this same stuff in my microwave," Maggie commented wryly as they finished dinner.

Gathered in the dining alcove, her fellow astronauts chuckled.

"You don't cook?" Adam asked.

"Do you know any single women who do?"

"I believe the married men have it over the rest of us," Grigg intoned. He made every statement sound like an immutable law of the universe. "Couples, families in particular, have much more traditional eating habits than the, uh—"

"The young and the restless?" Maggie put in.

"Uh, yes."

"What about you, Commander?" Maggie did everything but bat her eyelashes at him. She still chafed at Hal's suggestion that she "check him out." The man seemed perfectly normal. However, she owed the director a debt for getting her so much time in space. "Do you enjoy space-age cuisine?"

"I'd prefer a steak and a beer," he said.

"You'll get no argument there," Major Wells replied.

"I wonder if there's a way to cook food longer up here, not quicker," Maggie mused aloud. "To give the mouth-watering smells a chance to intensify instead of going up in steam the minute the lids are peeled off."

To Maggie's surprise a nostalgic smile softened Adam's features, until he caught her watching.

"We'd all come in from a hard day's work to the smells of dinner. I like the idea. But this is shoptalk for you. Anyone else working through dinner?"

Wells held up a hand. "I've got an assignment I'll need your help on."

"Sure."

"I'll clean up," Maggie offered.

"That's not your duty," Adam replied quietly.

"And don't I know it! I was raised with four brothers and, believe me, each and every one of them is capable of cooking, cleaning, and coaxing medication down a cat's throat. You all probably want to spend as much time as possible on your research. Believe it or not, the dining routine is part of mine."

"Can't argue with that." Joe Fontaine was ready to bolt at the word go.

"I second Fontaine," Wells replied.

When Grigg nodded, Adam did too. That quickly, the men scattered.

In the main room off the dining area Major Wells unsealed his orders, then requested coordinates be set to rendezvous with an object he neglected to specify. Dr. Grigg needed Adam's log entries deciphered. Joe Fontaine's experiments were so complex, Adam couldn't offer any assistance beyond directions to the top-deck botany lab, a self-contained Eden of over one hundred oxygen-producing plants, which was affectionately dubbed Botany Bay.

Maggie puttered until her turn came.

"I suppose you're next." Adam returned warily to the table. "What can I do for you, Ms. Mullins?"

Maggie explained away the tremor in her hands: It wasn't every day a woman faced down a lion in his den. "I believe you know why I'm here."

" 'To analyze the effects of prolonged solitude in an encapsulated environment—' "

She held up her palm, halting his by-the-book rendition of her mission. "That means you."

He slid into the booth. "I take it studying me from the ground is out?" He hitched his head toward the overhead camera mounted on the far wall.

"Observation is no substitute for experience."

"Never has been."

If only he knew, she thought, rapping the table with her knuckles. "What do you think of this?"

"It's a table."

"It folds down like an ironing board." Maggie grinned. "Is it useful?"

He shrugged. "We can eat without it."

"But isn't it more pleasant this way? A table means home, togetherness. It should foster team feeling among the crew."

He leaned back and folded his arms across his chest, the muscles in his arms clearly defined. "The psychology of inanimate objects."

"And how people react to them."

He nodded, more in assessment than agreement, as he scrutinized her from head to waist—everything that showed above the table.

Tabletops had another advantage, Maggie quickly realized. Like a lap bar on a roller coaster, they kept you from floating right up out of your seat.

She cleared her throat. "What I wanted to point out was how much our environment affects us emotionally. On a very subliminal level."

"Is that what this feeling is?" He leered at her.

At least, she *thought* it was a leer.

He laughed dryly. "I would have said having extra people aboard fosters team feeling. Tables don't do it."

"So this does nothing for you."

He quirked his mouth into a smile, staring at her openly. "I'd say it's the company, not the furniture."

"Ah." She glanced quickly around the room. Considering the atmosphere, neither one of them could stride, pace, or plant their feet. Too bad. She crossed her arms and leaned back in unconscious imitation of him.

Adam's laugh was husky and short. "Sorry if I just blew your theory."

"You haven't. Really. You've had real experience; that's what counts."

"Am I more experienced than you?" he asked softly, suggestively.

"In space travel, yes."

"Oh, that."

"Yes, that," she said, a little put out. She'd never been one to pout over a dismantled theory. In fact, there was a bright side to almost everything. "Six weeks will be invaluable as far as my own experience is concerned. I'll check my own reactions."

"To whom?" His eyes twinkled.

"To the ship." Maggie's cheeks burned flaming red. "Let's get on with it, shall we?"

He raised a brow in simulated shock. "Now? Here?"

"Commander, you know why I'm here."

"Maybe Hal sent me a birthday present after all."

Enough was enough. "I want to ask you a few questions. Important questions."

"I'm thirty-nine today, five foot ten, one hundred eighty pounds, although weight doesn't matter here. I don't think I'd be too heavy."

"For what?"

His eyes widened in imitation of hers. "Not the answers you had in mind?"

"Commander, I'm not here to dally with you. Or provoke, or tease, or entice."

"Or please, or excite, or coax, or stimulate?"

"No!"

"Excuse me, then."

"I hoped our first conversation would be less of a confrontation."

"Cut to the chase, sweetheart; you're here to keep an eye on me. You're going to ask pointed questions and transmit any disturbing answers straight to Hal. As far as I'm concerned, that's exactly where you can go."

He was as blunt as a dull razor and as angry as a panther teased in his cage.

Maggie chose her next words with utmost care. "That is not my primary purpose, I assure you. If you'd give me a chance . . ."

Adam sighed and ran a hand over his face, wondering for the umpteenth time why the hell he'd thought it necessary to shave before dinner because a woman was on board. "I didn't mean to bite your head off. It's just that I'm not cracking up and I'm not about to. I've been run through every test NASA can devise. Why Hal thought you'd find out anything new by coming here—"

"I have my own work."

"Ergonomics? Tell me that handy psychology degree had nothing to do with this six-week assignment."

"I never intended to psychoanalyze you. Please believe me."

When she said it in such a way—eyes a limpid, mossy brown; mouth soft and yielding—he almost did. Except believing women was part of what had driven him there in the first place. He'd been played for a sap before. "If I couldn't take the isolation, I'd know. You've heard the phrase 'Test pilots test themselves'?"

"Page one of the training manual. Your quote, I believe?"

His accomplishments were beside the point. "What I'm trying to say is, I've been tested under the weather, over the weather, and between the sheets. If Hal thinks I'm capable of running this mission, I'm capable of going to Mars. Report complete. Go shrink someone else."

Maggie suspected those were the most words he'd strung together in a month. "I wouldn't dream of shrinking you, Commander. Or enlarging you or widening you or altering you in any way." She batted her lashes again and flashed him a dazzling smile. Two could play the teasing game. "If you're done with your speech, may we get on with my study?"

He grudgingly planted his elbows on the table. "Shoot." He looked as if he expected her to pull a gun and do just that.

Calmly, she opened her journal and slid a piece of paper across to him. "Twenty questions," she replied. "Which parts of the ship do you feel most at ease in? Which areas do you retreat to when you need to concentrate? Where do you feel most calm, agitated, bored, stimulated?"

The last word won her a quick glare. He wriggled on the seat and deliberated over the questionnaire.

"There are five responses to each question, plus a blank for personal comments."

He plucked a pencil from his shirt pocket and got to work, marking boxes only, filling in no personal comments until he came to the second to last question. Maggie had tossed in one multiple choice guaranteed to show whether a subject was paying attention.

"What would you call a man who marries six times: (a) a bigamist, (b) a trigamist, (c) a sexgamist?"

Adam wrote in a hasty retort. *An optimist.* "That it?" His tart question startled the smile right off her face.

"Hardly." She exhaled, extracting another form. "Personal inventory next."

His palm hit the table with a smack. "I knew it."

"Different personalities react to their surroundings differently."

"You are analyzing me."

"Except for the fact that you're being difficult, I assure you I'm not."

"You could live here a year and know me no better than you do now."

"We have six weeks."

"Six years wouldn't make any difference. People barely know themselves, much less anyone else."

"Anyone or any woman?"

"Cute." He awarded her that one with a nod of his head. "Even Freud gave up on figuring women out."

Had Adam given up? Maggie wondered. "I think men being mystified by women goes all the way back to the original Adam."

"It hasn't stopped with this one."

"The mission to Mars will last three long years. It's not too much to ask that the living quarters be as comfortable as possible, as conducive to efficient scientific pursuit as we can make them."

Adam huffed. "Is that the speech that got you here?"

Maggie flushed and forced the corners of her mouth into a professional smile. "I've been defending my work almost from its inception. Environment is vital to the psychological well-being of the crew."

"So you want to make this place homey."

"I want to make it human."

"With tables? Paint samples? What next, wood paneling and brass fittings on the portholes? You could turn it into Captain Nemo's sub."

He already had, she thought, the idea striking her out of the blue. Instead of being "twenty thousand leagues under the sea," Adam was twenty thousand leagues above and just as isolated. She got back to work. "Do you like your quarters? How about your bedroom?"

"How about it?"

"I noticed you haven't done much to beautify it."

"I put you in it."

She caught her breath for a moment, then expelled it with a tiny laugh. "I meant photos. Memorabilia."

"I've been in the military a long time. I like it neat."

"Soldiers in World War One decorated their fox-holes. In Vietnam they pinned symbols to their helmets."

"Then let's say I don't like clutter."

"Physical or emotional?"

Adam studied her hard. "If you're not a shrink—"

She bit her tongue. Why didn't she hit the eject button and get it over with? "I'm not. I'm curious." The least she could do was look him straight in the eye.

His eyes were dark with renewed suspicion. "So if your job isn't to analyze me, tell me something about you."

Fair enough. Maggie took a deep breath and rose to the challenge. "I'm thirty, unmarried, and have two science degrees, which you know about, since you read my file."

His mouth quirked again, and his eyes softened in masculine appreciation.

"I have four brothers, all in science-related fields. As for me, I've designed everything from motor homes to prison cells to college dormitories. The tighter the space, the more important the design. Although the cells weren't done with comfort in mind," she amended quickly. "For that matter, neither were the dorms."

They both laughed. Good. If there was anything Maggie excelled at, it was making men comfortable. "I've wanted to come here for a long time. To test the quarters myself, see how things are working out. And to meet you."

"And if I tell you I'm happy with the place?"

"You won't get rid of me that easily." The man had a hundred admirers and very few friends. She decided right there to be one of the few.

Baby sister to four brothers in a house without a mother, she keyed in quickly on men's insecurities, the kind they didn't show women they wanted to impress.

Not that she hadn't had her share of attention. Men

had tried. Men had failed. Or rather, Maggie had failed and men had lost interest. She'd spare Adam that part. All she wanted was to gain his confidence and learn what made him tick—not at Hal's urging, but for her own peace of mind. After all, how could she make a home for a man she didn't know?

"I brought some things with me," she said eagerly. "For you." She pulled a George Jones tape out of one of the zippered pockets in her slacks. "Thought you'd be getting tired of the ones you packed."

"Thanks."

"You're welcome. Hal sent some too. And don't let me forget this." She handed him a sealed birthday card.

Adam saw the writing. "From Tad," he said. His feelings for his stepson were obviously intense and private. "Thanks. I'll open it later."

"I did read some of your file." She'd given it a cursory speed-read in Hal's office. But when Maggie cared, she was as curious as a cat. "Tell me a little about Tad."

"It's his birthday, too, his nineteenth." He tapped the card against his fingertips, watching her carefully. "I always told his father he gave me a godson for my birthday."

Maggie smiled wistfully. "You never knew you'd get him permanently."

Adam scowled. "You've heard the story."

"I've also heard you were more helpful."

"Being flexible is part of my job."

"Flexible enough to put aside a happy bachelorhood to raise another man's son?" She asked it as gently as she could. It was clear he still hurt over it.

Adam Strade had plainly steeled himself to the pain a long time ago. It wasn't something to flaunt or dredge up, except perhaps on long nights alone.

"I'm not asking to analyze you, honestly. I thought you might like to talk."

The radio crackled. "Mission Control to Space Station McAuliffe. Mission Control to McAuliffe."

Maggie stiffened as a chill ran down her spine.

"Radio bother you?" Adam asked, eyeing her closely.

"Last time I heard that voice, we were about to launch. That's the man who sent me into space."

"The only one?" He gave a short laugh at her startled look and got up to answer the call. But when the transmission was finished, she was waiting, supposedly so they could "just talk."

Adam eased an ache nagging at the back of his neck. He didn't like being so cynical or so tired. For a year he'd been more or less alone. Talking to Maggie would be as much fun as probing a bruise, but there was little alternative. Hal wanted Adam's emotions examined. It'd be easier and quicker to simply hand the lady his psyche on a silver platter. If he was lucky, she'd learn what she needed and go home with the others.

"Have a seat. Or a hover." She smiled.

He grumbled rather than grinned. The woman irritated him like fine sandpaper, getting under his skin with a sweetness that almost passed for innocence—and a guardedness that almost matched his. It was a classic catch-22: When he flirted, she ran; when he ran, she turned around and pursued.

"Tad's father was killed and I adopted his son and married his widow. Is that what you wanted to hear?" He took his seat again, resting his elbows on the table before reaching across to unclench her hands.

"Uh, Commander, what exactly are you doing?"

He raised his brows innocently, a smile flitting about in the deep crinkles around his eyes. "Holding your hands."

"Why?"

"So we stay anchored."

"The table will do that."

"I believe in backup systems."

"Are you backing me up? Or backing me off?"

He pursed his lips and looked at their joined hands.

"I've noticed, Commander, you flirt most outrageously when you want to distract me."

"And I've noticed you call me Commander when my flirting works. Does it bother you? Tell me how you feel about that."

She smiled, a twitch really, acknowledging his imitation of a psychoanalyst.

"Think of it as a lie detector," he added helpfully, folding her fingers in his fist. "You can measure my tension as I answer."

Measuring tension worked both ways, she thought, fighting to keep her hand relaxed as he squeezed lightly. Embers of awareness should *not* be shooting through her nervous system, she told herself. Despite the mental red alert, her hand grew warm in his just the same.

When he began to talk, his voice was grainy and rough.

"Todd Donnelly and I were in 'Nam together. He was twenty-five, a pilot. I was a scared-witless navigator of nineteen who got the rare honor of taking over the controls one day when Todd's arm got shot up."

"He talked you down?"

"Before passing out from loss of blood, yeah. One of those war stories you read about, strictly out of channels and too good to be true."

"What happened then?"

"I followed him around like a lost puppy who'd been fed steak. He was married, his son just born. He made me promise to look after the kid if anything happened to him. When he re-upped Stateside to test jets, I came along. He taught me to be careful."

"You? Careful?"

His grin didn't entirely hide his pride. "Yeah, well, I've been known to take my spins."

"And take a few unauthorized personnel on night flights over Hudson Bay."

He grimaced. "Is that what it says in the file?"

Disgruntled at revealing how thoroughly she remembered the paperwork Hal had shown her, she quoted the passage. "'Unauthorized female personnel.'"

"Somebody authorized them to be female, all right. The sad fact was, they weren't allowed in some of the fancier hardware we tested out."

"'Showed off' might be more like it."

He grinned a sassy, saucy, know-it-all grin that was sure to have gotten him in with, and in trouble with, more than one commanding officer. "Showed them what the machinery could do," he corrected her.

Yes, but whose machinery? she thought. "Then what?"

"Do I have to tell you that part too?"

He was throwing her looks that should have had her bouncing off the opposite bulkhead. "I meant later in your life, Commander."

"When are you going to call me Adam?"

When he stopped holding her hands, she thought. Unfortunately, he obeyed her unspoken wish. Withdrawing, he tightened his arms across his torso, thinking the next part out thoroughly before he spoke.

"Ten years later Todd was killed." Is that what she wanted to hear? Probably. Like ripping off a bandage, it was better to do it quick. "He went down outside Edwards Air Force Base testing an F-20. First time I landed the shuttle, the scorch marks were still there. Tad was ten, I was twenty-nine, and Julie was the grieving widow. She needed someone." He stated the last part as if he didn't care who believed him. "I married her."

"It lasted eight years, and you've been divorced two."

He looked her in the eye and took her hand,

damned if he knew why. Maybe it was the glimmer of pink in her cheeks, the awareness that said she knew, and he knew, what a simple touch could mean. And what it could lead to.

He ran his thumb over her palm, intrigued to find it slightly damp under his pressure. "You're thinking it," he demanded softly. "Ask it."

She moistened her lips first with a quick flick of her tongue. "Did you love her?" This time Maggie laced her fingers through his and held on. "Adam, tell me."

"I promised Todd I'd take care of them. I didn't promise that a week after the funeral I'd be in the sack with his wife."

"That's very harsh."

"That's exactly how she put it. Julie had a way of being blunt about a man's shortcomings."

It seemed to hit her right between the eyes. She blinked a couple of times. "How could any woman—?"

He stopped her with a look. "I'll take that as a compliment, but you didn't know Julie. She could turn a good deed into something that ate at a man."

Adam got up and moved around, shoulders hunched as if a ghost trailed him. Eight years of being confounded, of trying to make things work but nevertheless failing a woman, and he still wasn't sure what had gone wrong. "I wasn't the man Todd was, and she made sure I knew it."

But it had played both ways. Julie wasn't the woman he thought he'd known all those years. If he didn't know his best friend's wife well enough to marry her, how could he know any woman? Trust one? Trust his own fool judgment?

He looked at Maggie a long while. She wasn't filling the silence for him this time. "Talk about crash and burn. The day after Tad's seventeenth birthday I bailed out."

Maggie bowed her head. He flung the words at her,

tossing out information the way a sinking ship ditches ballast. It didn't lighten his load.

"I did a decent job of raising the boy. Despite everything, I don't regret that."

Maggie glanced at the bright-red birthday card in his hand. Doing his duty. Fulfilling a promise. Old standbys for a man with Adam Strade's sense of honor. Hadn't Julie Donnelly seen what a good man she'd had? Had the woman been blind or just grief stricken? That excuse might have worked for the first few months of their marriage, but later . . .

Maggie knew she had to back off—she was getting too distracted by visions of sitting down with Mrs. Strade and giving her a talking-to about knowing a good man when she saw one. She chewed a thumbnail while Adam threw switches on the console, signing off for the night.

Turning in might be the best idea of all; she was exhausted. Rising from the table, she edged toward the hall, waiting for him to finish. "You must be proud of what you did for Tad."

Proud? He was nuts. One minute he wanted Maggie Mullins off his space station and out of his life, the sooner the better. The next, things were pouring out, things he rarely talked about, especially with a woman. "Hope you didn't mind the maudlin parts."

"Not at all."

"I'm not fond of sob stories. You're too easy to talk to." He said it as if he weren't sure he approved of it.

"Men tell me that a lot." She laughed. "I'm like a kid sister."

"I picture some cowboy giving you the same sad song in a bar somewhere. Some country-and-western place up Fort Worth way."

"You have a vivid imagination."

"Would it work?"

She laughed again. Adam swayed, inhaling the tantalizing scent released every time she tossed that mane of red hair.

"I'm a sucker for a sad song," she said.

And he was a sucker, plain and simple. His palm tingled just beneath the skin when he touched her, stopping her at the doorway to his room. "We could have a few beers."

"Here?"

"In Fort Worth sometime."

Her smile indulged him. "Maybe sometime."

"We'll dance a bit, walk outside when it gets too smoky, look up at the stars." He would lean her up against a pickup truck and kiss her senseless. Then they'd be even. "Can you picture that, Maggie?"

Maggie gulped. His mouth, she'd just noticed, was nothing remarkable. It was a man's mouth, the lips neither thick nor thin, not meanly slashed nor sensuously full. Not the kind of mouth to bring long, slow kisses to mind at all. So why did she feel the wall at her back so keenly? Why was she imagining what his arms would feel like winding around her in a parking lot under the stars?

Three

"The stars," she repeated, aware she'd been silent too long.

"I can show them to you."

They stood in front of the door to his room. He opened it.

Doors didn't lock on space stations. Maggie would have to keep that in mind when the rest of the crew returned to Earth in four days and she was alone with Adam Strade.

The light came on automatically. He reached in and shut it off.

"I don't usually enter dark bedrooms with men after knowing them all of eight hours." Maggie tried to chuckle, her heartbeat rocketing so hard, she swore it echoed off the walls.

"It's the view I want you to see." He pushed up a built-in shade.

The words died in her mouth. "Oh, Adam."

Stars and more stars glittered through the heavens, bright, blinding, and breath-stealing. A billion came to mind, for once having nothing to do with the national debt. "Where does it end?"

"It doesn't. That's what eternity looks like."

Suddenly his wish to crowd her, to get a rise out of her, maybe even to lure her and try his luck vanished. The awe and reverence on her face struck something deep inside him. "I felt that way the first time I saw it too. I have you to thank for that."

"I can't take credit for *this*!"

"You got us the extra portholes. You're keeping astronauts sane, Maggie. And motivated. Every time I look out that window, I know why I'm here." And every time he looked at her, he forgot why she was there.

The woman was analyzing him, sure as those stars burned in the sky. She had the power to confine him to Earth or pronounce him fit to go to Mars. And he was mixed up enough to be thinking of kisses.

So he wanted to touch her; that was normal, wasn't it? She was a beautiful woman; they were alone in his room. Her rose scent already permeated the air. How long would it last when she was gone? he wondered.

Besides, he argued with himself, if she *was* a shrink, she'd draw the line at kisses. Which meant stopping wasn't his problem; it was hers.

So there was urgency. And lust. And a throat-tightening gratitude for her simply being a woman, thinking like one, caring like one.

Gratitude, hell. When she parted her lips, he knew they'd passed gratitude a quarter orbit ago.

"Adam, it's magnificent." She sighed, watching the infinite dots of light.

Starlight alone lit the room, throwing two shadows on the wall. It was strange, starlight. Like moonlight it bleached away color. But not hers. Her pale skin glowed softly with excitement. Her eyes sparkled, alight at the vastness of it all.

Pulses of energy thrummed around them, the electronic hum of the ship itself as solar panels deployed. Stars burned like torches in the velvet empty blackness. And a living, breathing woman laughed in delight and sighed once more. Could Adam coax her into turning and looking at him with the same wonder? Maybe. If he had the nerve to touch her.

Nerve had never been Adam's problem. Test pilots had it in spades. His failure was plain common sense where women were concerned. He appreciated them, respected them, but ever since Julie, he'd been convinced he'd never understand them. He could live with that. From a distance.

Maggie gradually caught on. They were alone. In his bedroom. "I, uh, feel a little light-headed. Do you think that's from the weightlessness?"

"Could be. The heart pounds in funny ways up here." His was. He touched the pulse on the side of her neck. "Mind if I show you?"

There was something extremely erotic about giving someone permission to touch you, Maggie thought. The mind agreed to what the body yearned for as they drifted continually closer.

"Consider it a scientific experiment," he chided gently, as if sensing her self-consciousness. He reached in under the shadow of her long hair and touched her skin.

A long moment passed.

Gravity wasn't the only thing making her float. Inside, everything turned liquid; flares shot up like sunspots when he trailed his fingertips lightly down her throat. He placed his hands on her shoulders, gently nudging her downward until her face aligned with his.

"I never imagined so many stars," she said, catching their reflection in his eyes.

"Have you ever imagined this?" He brushed her lips with his. They parted with his name.

He took advantage, touching her teeth with his tongue, running his hands down her arms. Both of them aware of the body warmth captured in the folds of her sweater. But only Maggie knew the heat building next to her skin, the flush spreading between her breasts.

She touched his chest, flattened her palms there. He didn't budge. In a moment she wasn't sure she wanted him to. He tasted so earthy, so real, so alone. She wanted to ease his loneliness, to reach out to him. It was within her grasp, as simple as her fingers wrapping around his biceps.

Her body bumped his. Unintentionally. Almost innocently. And she sought his lips again.

Whatever he'd sought, he'd discovered the first time around. Now he took her farther. He grasped her to him, making sure she felt the hard, undeniable consequences of beckoning a man to unburden his secrets in the dark.

She gasped at her answering rush of sensation.

The intercom crackled like static. "Commander, please report to the bridge." Major Wells's voice.

"Damn." Adam held her away from him, looking out over her head to the blazing stars before peering into her doe-wide eyes. "Forgot we had company." He ran a thumb over her lips and left. That would have to do for an apology.

Maggie bounced lightly against the bulkhead. She would have sunk happily to the floor and rolled herself into a fetal position if she'd been able to. Instead she merely tucked up her knees and wrapped her arms around them, right there in midair.

Where Adam Strade had left her.

She listened to his faraway replies, grunted responses to technical questions about setting their coordinates for the night. Wells thanked him. Maggie's heart jumped. She reached for the door. Nothing happened. She frowned, shoved off from the wall at her back, and bounded across the room.

He heard the thump as he came down the gangway. "You okay?"

"I think I'll turn in." Clutching the doorjamb, she blocked the entrance. This was going to be very strange indeed if she couldn't hear his footsteps in the hall. "I may write up some notes."

"Sure." He didn't get frosty. He was too subtle for that, too used to command to show all of his emotions. "I was going to explain the sleeping routine to the rest of the crew and turn in myself."

"Ah. Good."

"Mind if I come in and get the rest of my things?"

"Sure."

"Good."

He edged past, filling a knapsack with another shirt, a pair of pants, and what toiletries he hadn't already taken.

"You forgot your razor," she said, handing him the electric. "I kind of glanced around earlier." That would have to do for a confession, she thought.

He opened the underwear drawer, then packed a pair of socks. "Glad you're getting oriented," he said.

"Sure am."

"Right. I'll be at the end of the hall, third sleeping bag on your left. Grigg and Fontaine will sleep a later shift, and Wells will man the bridge during the night. Call me if you need anything."

She nodded, sliding the door shut behind him. Those stars would burn out quicker than she'd call him back.

She had notes to compile. And a kiss to explain. In writing.

Adam made his way down the hall to turn in.

Supposedly, he had his answer. No psychiatrist would kiss a patient the way she had kissed him. And no responsible space station commander would kiss a crew-woman the same way.

He cursed blackly. If Hal hadn't sent her to check on him, he didn't know Hal. Hal was worried. Hal thought he was hiding. Adam wasn't so sure himself—not after his instant attraction to a woman he should have kept at arm's length.

He ran a hand through his hair, wincing at how long it had become. Appearances. How deceptive were they?

Take Maggie Mullins. Please. The woman was delightful and spontaneous and didn't mind tumbling through space her first day without gravity.

On the other hand, she blushed like a sun-kissed peach when he turned on his minor-league charm.

On the other hand, she'd stood up for work no one else took seriously, because she believed it would make a difference to the people on this station.

On the other hand, she'd kissed him back.

"Hell, Strade, any more hands and you're gonna look like one of Grigg's mice."

So how did he convince her and Hal he was well adjusted enough to stand up to three more years in space? "Not by jumping all over the lady like some shipwrecked sailor," he muttered. "Like *Robinson Crusoe on Mars*."

She wasn't the first woman assigned to a shuttle crew. Only the first he'd reacted to so strongly.

Why? Because she'd responded to his story with emotion as well as logic. Because she'd looked at those stars the way he did when no one was around to see it. It had been a long time since a woman had reached for his heart instead of his body.

A long, long time since he'd let one find it.

What was she up to?

He unzipped his sleeping bag. A note floated out from under the pillow.

Sloping handwriting drifted before him. *I forgot to say Happy Birthday, Commander. Many, many more.* She'd signed it M&M and had pinned a bag of chocolate candies to the pillowcase.

The woman knew his weaknesses. Exactly what he was afraid of.

• • •

"Mission Control to Space Station McAuliffe," the intercom crackled. "Come in, McAuliffe."

"Ah, Houston, we have a situation here," Adam said in a raspy voice, emotions rigorously under control. "Do you read me, Houston?"

Even at five A.M. Mission Control hummed with activity. That activity quieted instantly as Adam's terse message came over the speakers.

"Reading you, McAuliffe. Specify situation, please."

Maggie bit her lip, tension thickening in the airless compartment of the crowded bridge. Grigg pressed in beside her. Major Wells peered over her shoulder at the snowy television screen showing the tiers of consoles at Mission Control.

"Houston," Adam said, voice harsh. "Dr. Grigg informs me we have a problem. There's a . . . a rampant mutational anomaly on board."

The first response from Houston was increased static, then Hal's familiar, resolutely unexcitable voice. "Uh, exactly what form does this anomaly take, Commander?"

"In other words, what the hell's going on?" Joe Fontaine blurted out, startling everyone gathered on the bridge. "Make him tell you that, why don't you?"

Strade squinted at Fontaine. "Settle down, kid."

"Stop calling me kid! I have a Ph.D., I know a disaster when I see one, and this one's growing!"

Grigg, demonstrating total disdain for Joe's panicky outburst, leaned over and grasped the microphone. A tussle broke out as Joe tried to pull it away. Wells maneuvered between them.

"If you won't tell them, I will," Joe shouted.

"That does it," Adam yelled. "Fontaine, back to your quarters!"

"I'm not going back there! That *thing's* back there!"

"Off the bridge!" Adam's voice thundered. "Now!"

Maggie didn't envy the recipient of Adam's look. They were all unsteadily balanced between hysteria and calm, relying on Adam to set the tone.

"Commander Strade," the radio hissed, "come in. Come in, Strade. Define situation, please."

As Fontaine retreated the remaining four considered the camera mounted over the exit to the hallway. Then they exchanged glances, all eyes coming to rest on Adam.

Maggie heard the scrape of beard as he ran a hand tiredly over his cheek and turned back to the console.

Three indistinct figures had gathered around their own screen in Houston, the poor transmission showing only their white shirts and dark ties. One of them was Hal. Suddenly the atmospheric interference disappeared, and his voice came through loud and clear. "Adam, what the hell is going on?"

"Sorry, Hal. It appears one of Grigg's experiments got out of hand."

"Out of hand?" Maggie squawked. "There's a creature on board!"

Adam compressed his lips, gripping the microphone tighter. "Unfortunately, the lady's correct."

"Come again?"

Grigg easily muscled Adam aside in the zero gravity, a move Maggie doubted he'd have dared on Earth, or under any circumstances less desperate than these.

Grigg cleared his throat. "One of my subjects has undergone some as yet unidentified genetic disturbance of a cellular molecular origination. Consequently, it is exhibiting signs of unwarranted gross exaggeration of features normally associated with— with creatures of a much larger size."

"We've been required to shut down the lower science lab," Adam added. "We've cut off all oxygen to the thing, but it hasn't had any effect."

The dark ties leaned toward their consoles. Then

the men all glanced up. Maggie realized she and the crew of the space station, minus Fontaine, were now on the big screen in Houston. She forced herself to show as little response as possible. It wasn't easy. A hushed silence reigned over the cabin as Adam traded looks with each of them.

"Are you telling us," Hal repeated slowly, "that you have a giant mouse on board?"

Adam's control snapped. "Mouse, hell! It's the size of a small rhino, and it's loose in my space lab!"

"I believe," Grigg corrected, "that it's more the size of a large marsupial. The mouse family is after all—"

"Can it, Grigg! You've gotten us in enough trouble. Houston, I realize this is an unprecedented event," Adam stated.

"Unprecedented event?" Maggie gasped. "Can't you come up with a better euphemism than that? We've got a creature on board!"

Adam's shoulders tensed, but he refused to turn away from the screen. "Houston, we've been trying to switch on the camera to the science bay from here so you can see for yourself. That's not working either."

"We'll try it from down here, Commander. We'll relay transmission; you should get it in a second."

In a moment the picture appeared on the console. Maggie let out a stifled squeak and clamped her hand over her mouth. Adam gave her a warning scowl. On the screen a massive rodent twitched, its nose pressed disgustingly to the glass, whiskers quivering over reddish eyes, tail swatting a pale flesh-color growth on its ribs.

"What is that on its side?" Hal asked, the hush from Mission Control complete.

"I don't know," Adam lied.

"At this point I can only hypothesize," Grigg tried weakly. "It may be mutating before our eyes. This is an advance none of us was prepared for. You have to admit, gentlemen, whatever else this is, it's an exciting day for science—"

Maggie grasped his arm. "Doctor, please."

"He's right," Adam said, averting his eyes from the hideous sight on the console screen, staring fixedly at Maggie as he spoke. His words were heavy with portent. "Whatever the danger to ourselves, we may be noting this day on our calendars for some time to come."

On the screen the gigantic rodent squirmed, biting at what looked suspiciously like a human thumb. "Ouch," a voice said.

It took ten excruciating seconds before bursts of laughter cascaded over the airwaves from Houston.

"April Fool's," Maggie and Adam shouted in unison, Wells and Grigg not far behind. Fontaine popped out from behind the mouse, his own nose gargantuan when he pressed it to the science bay camera, then he pushed off the wall and waved.

"Strade, we'll have your stripes for this!" Hal declared.

"You'll have to beat off my killer rodent to get them."

More laughter bounced off the satellite transmission.

"Congratulations, Dr. Grigg," Hall said sarcastically, "I see you're growing bigger and better jackasses up there."

Adam and Grigg exchanged high fives upside down. Wells clapped Maggie on the back, laughing harder as she shot across the cabin.

"Whoa!" Adam grasped her arm as she sailed by.

"Like my joke?" she asked, when their laughter finally subsided.

"Very much." His appreciative look said more than that. Her humor wasn't the only thing he liked about Maggie Mullins. She'd given him few chances to show it these last couple of days.

"Excuse me, I have to make some notes."

"Sure." He let her slide away, the lack of gravity allowing her to slink out of his reach as subtly as an undersea nymph. "Look out for mutating rodents."

She laughed. "I will."

Saying little, asking less, she'd attempted no further interviews with him since that first night. Maybe she'd given up trying to get inside his head. Maybe she'd leave with the rest of the crew the following morning; he'd been dropping hints to no discernible effect. He was perfectly willing to forgo her company if it meant regaining his peace of mind.

Until he found himself following her down the passageway. "About that episode the other night . . ."

"Adam, please."

"Okay, so I get lonely. A little too much talk, some physical contact, let's say I overreacted and I'm sorry."

"That's very considerate of you." Too much so. His approach required overlooking *her* reaction as well.

Her lips throbbed each time she thought of that kiss, her dreams echoed with it, and her cheeks colored whenever she dared look him in the eye. Problem was, he seemed determined to block the passageway until she did.

"Adam, I believe we can successfully put that behind us. It was uncharacteristic of us both."

"You talked to Hal on the radio yesterday. I saw the transmission log."

"You don't miss much."

He missed her. He saw her chatting with the others, interviewing them, handing out those questionnaires, and he missed the contact. Not that he planned opening up to her like he had the first night, but surely she had enough on him to take back to Houston by now.

The thought brought a frown to his face. "You're leaving, then."

"Good heavens, no."

"Then what were you talking to Hal about? The kiss?"

Her gaze flickered away as Grigg excused himself and glided between them on his way to the lab.

"I told Hal exactly what I've told you all along," she said when they were alone again. "I'm not a psychiatrist, and what's more, we're too close up here to conduct any kind of official analysis."

"Then your mission is over."

"I need to live here for my study. I'm sure we can maintain some semblance of professional behavior if we work at it."

He touched her hair. "How can you return to someplace you've never been?"

The move was designed to fool her every bit as much as the mouse had fooled Hal. He'd get close, scare her away. Angels with mossy brown eyes didn't belong in one-man monasteries. After one kiss she'd retreated for two days. Maybe another would unnerve her for good.

"Maggie," he said, scaling his fingertips over her cheek.

It scared her, all right. Right into her room. The door slid shut with a decisive thump. "We'll keep this professional."

"The uses of humor," Maggie wrote, comfortably squeezed into a corner of her room, her journal resting on her knee, a smile hovering on her lips. It had taken her twenty minutes of deep breathing and slow stretching, but her heartbeat was normal now and her mind clear. She focused solely on the morning's practical joke.

(1) It relieves tension. And there'd certainly been enough of that between her and the commander.

(2) Shared fun builds relationships. Not that she was thinking of anything like a relationship in refer-

ence to Adam Strade. They'd all played a part, shared a laugh at the expense of their employer. And Adam, despite his reputation as a loner, had taken the lead.

(3) Pranks are a gentle way of retaliating against constant observation. His stroke of genius had been using Houston's camera to fool Houston into thinking they had a mouse the size of a house on board.

Maggie chuckled again, then got serious. Involving everyone in a whimsical conspiracy might be somewhat calculated, but she hoped her practical joke had practical consequences—*i.e., emphasizing friendship of a nonsexual kind with Adam Strade.*

If that look in his eye was any indication, she'd failed. Talk about interacting. Her heart pounded double time just to think of it. He looked at her as if they'd been made for each other.

Despite her brothers' assurances that she'd find the right guy sooner or later, there seemed to be very few men made with Maggie Mullins in mind.

She was too tall, with the wide shoulders of a swimmer and the long legs of a runway model. Since those legs came attached to a slim-hipped, well-toned body, she got a lot of initial interest—but little more.

Not for the first time she wondered if the assertiveness a girl learned living with four brothers scared men off. Ditto talent, intelligence, and a complete lack of feminine instinct.

"Feminine wiles," Maggie murmured. She'd never owned a set and couldn't specifically define them unless batting one's lashes and wiggling one's hips was the way to a man's heart.

And yet somehow she'd captured Adam Strade's attention.

"You're the only woman in the galaxy, that's why." And the following day she'd be the only other person on board.

"Think quick. What's guaranteed to turn a man off?"

"Sleeping with you," a voice answered from deep

inside, reverberating like a slap. Or a dose of badly needed reality.

Maggie put down her pencil and rubbed her eyes, sighing in defeat as it floated carelessly away. "I meant short of sleeping with him."

She would spare him that trauma. She'd be honored to be his friend, that's all. Any more than that, and she was doomed to fail.

"Mind explaining the silent treatment?"

"As I've told you before, don't pay any attention to me."

It was her eighth day on board and their fourth day alone. Maggie floated on the periphery as Adam went about his daily duties.

He fed the mice. She watched from a corner.

He logged what the animals ate, how much water they drank, if they used their little wheels. She scribbled.

He contacted satellites in this portion of their orbit, observed meteorological developments on Earth, even did laundry. He offered to wash hers.

"Pretend I'm not even here."

After four days of her hovering, Adam was ready to break down and tell her anything if only she'd stop playing guardian angel. "Was it something I said?"

A soft chuckle emanated from the upper right corner of the room. "I'm not here to converse; I'm here to observe. Like a fly on the wall."

He looked her up and down, mostly up, from navy slippers to aqua slacks to an aqua turtleneck covered caressingly by a crocheted vest. It was a daisy pattern, attractive but hardly sexy, unless the woman wearing it was Maggie Mullins.

Two of those daisies pressed subtly forward; Adam easily imagined the pert breasts behind them. Three buttons barely hung on in their laggard buttonholes, just waiting to be parted, opened, spread . . .

Higher up, her red hair fluffed around her head, a strawberry-gold halo thick enough to trap a man's hands, the face it framed delicate enough to make those hands pause. He had run a thumb over those lips, pursed in concentration now, faintly outlined in pink. He had pressed them apart with his own.

A glittering gold stud of earring flashed, ready to click against his teeth were he to nuzzle her ear, tasting those faint freckles on her skin.

Her eyes were hazel-brown with green, flecked with gold and caution each time she caught him watching. He wanted a response, that was all.

"Pretend I'm a fly on the wall," she repeated firmly.

"Flies aren't built that way." He frankly appraised her body one more time. She shot him a scathing look. "They have compound eyes, for one thing," he muttered.

"Unlike Dr. Grigg's mice. You described them as if they were little monsters. They're actually perfectly normal."

"Want me to take one out of a cage and show you?"

"No! I mean, don't bother, really. I can see them from here."

"Like me?" he said after a short pause.

"Adam, this is necessary, honestly. I need to observe how you deal with being alone."

"But I'm not alone, am I?"

"We could overcome that if you'd cooperate a bit."

He kept a blunt expletive to himself. "There are a number of things a cooperative woman can do."

It wasn't entirely her fault he was working up a good case of the hots for her. It wasn't her fault he'd kissed her. Nor her fault she'd reacted the way she had. Heck, it had been her first night in space. She'd been unsteady, maybe a little needy.

And he'd been dumb enough to think he was what she'd needed. It wasn't the first time in his life that thought tripped him up.

But he had to hand it to her. After eight days in

space the lady was in complete control of her emotions, pleasantly watching him struggle with his.

"Tell you what," he grumbled, "come on down to the welcoming bay. You can watch me run on *my* little wheel."

Four

Maggie sighed. Watching Adam exercise today would no doubt be as disturbing as watching Adam exercise the day before and the day before that. He stood with his back to the wall, arms punching the air, resisting the coiled springs. His bare chest glistened. A smattering of crisp dark hair circled his nipples, outlined with a sheen of sweat.

"Join me?" he huffed, a saucy grin on his face.

She hadn't done so the previous day and she wouldn't now. "I'm fine over here."

"Take a glance at that," he said, nodding toward the left while throwing a right jab. "If you're going to be here awhile, you'll need to try some."

A chart on the wall explained various uses of the equipment. It wasn't exactly engrossing, but it was better than staring at his rippling chest or at the way he flexed his hand before throwing another punch.

He grunted some advice between sets. "Since so little effort . . . is required to move around . . . up here . . . you'll find you don't sleep . . . for long."

"I've slept very well." If getting up at five A.M. was considered very well.

"Any nightmares, you know where to find me."

"Thank you, Commander. I sleep fine."

"I can imagine."

She was sure he could. Maggie's own imagination worked overtime as she dreamed in her hammock of bunched muscles and compact powerful moves.

A Randy Travis song warmed the air. Adam liked music when he worked out. So did Maggie. It transported her to romantic places, like a barroom in Fort Worth, a parking lot where Adam Strade handed her up into his truck, looking proprietary, proud.

The music got louder. "There," he said.

She started. "You didn't have to turn that up for me."

"You were humming."

She laughed, hoping fantasies didn't show. "Was it that bad?"

Adam shook his head and went back to work. On the contrary, he thought, her humming was too good, too intimate. In his experience it was something women did while washing dishes, pinning up their hair, taking a bath. It was something Maggie did—and what stirred him was she didn't seem to notice it until he mentioned it. When he did, she stopped.

"Are you going to watch?" he asked, counting out the heartbeats until she answered, tightening the resistance on a stationary bike before he strapped himself on.

"I thought I'd go back to the kitchen area and jot down some notes."

"Maggie." He hadn't meant to call after her, not that quickly. "I thought you had to, uh, watch."

"I already know what you do in here."

"Sometimes I talk."

"Pardon?"

"To myself." Damn. He hadn't meant to make that sound so pitiful, although a small calculating corner of his soul reminded him that getting personal had softened her up before. "I'd rather talk to you." His voice was gruffer this time.

"That interview our first night—"

His mouth twitched in a smile at her phrasing. *Our first night.* He quickly squelched it.

"—I'm sorry I intruded on your privacy like that."

"And the silent treatment's supposed to make up for it?"

No, she thought, the pal treatment was. No more kisses. No more misleading a lonely man. "Please just follow your usual routine."

"But I can't, dammit. I know you've gotten it into that frizzy head of yours to be as remote as Hal in Houston, but you're here. How can a man not notice?"

She studiously flipped the pages of her notebook, clicking a little more lead into her mechanical pencil.

Adam winced. He'd raised his voice. He'd also said the wrong thing. How in heaven's name did women hurt so easy? And how exactly did men know it the minute they trespassed on sensitive territory? Damned if he knew. He wouldn't be in this position if he had the answers. "Look, I'm sorry I said your hair was frizzy."

"Hmm?" She looked up, completely nonchalant. "Did you say something?"

"Yes!" He brought his voice down a notch. A couple of notches. "You've got very pretty hair."

"Thank you. Carry on." She waved a hand at the exercise equipment.

"What would you call it?"

"Call what?"

"Your hair."

She shrugged and bobbed with the motion. "Have you ever heard of Burne-Jones?"

He ransacked his mind and came up with George Burns and George Jones. "No."

"He was a painter. Pre-Raphaelite. His models looked like this."

"Another degree in art history."

"A minor." She gave a quick apologetic shrug. "I guess frizzy pretty much covers the hair."

For a split second he had visions of it covering him—red, russet, warm, and gold. She usually tied it back in a wide ponytail. Today a big barrette with a chopstick poked through it anchored it at the nape of her neck.

She pulled the pencil out from where she'd stowed it next to her ear and jotted something else in her book.

What else could he talk to her about? He didn't want to appear too desperate or she'd write that down. If he came on too bawdy, she'd back away. The ironic part was, he had to get close to her to convince her he was sane enough to face another three years alone.

But hell, he was man enough to admit he got lonely sometimes. Why not go along with her questions? After all, he wasn't going to fall in love with the woman.

Maggie sipped coffee through a straw. Water didn't flow in space. Funny how awareness did. Ripples of consciousness reminded her of that every time Adam flexed a hand or turned toward a monitor.

The man had a way of making her pay attention with every raised hair on her arm, with each fluttering pulse. He damn near made her freckles dance. And all he was doing was staring at the Earth, apple-green and swirling blue, clouds strung across her middle in a cottony girdle.

"A high-pressure zone moving east over Asia Minor," he droned into the microphone. "Looks like snow for the Mongolians. I'll update you on the Philippine volcano in a few minutes as we come around."

The microwave pinged. Maggie hauled out the next course. She tore off the foil tops, hissing as steam burned her fingertips, and let the odors waft through the room. "It's on the table!"

Hal's voice crackled in the background. "Sounds like the little lady calling."

Adam grunted. "Let me finish the South Pacific first."

"You want caffeinated or decaffeinated?" she asked.

"Be there in a minute. I'm playing weatherman," he tacked on with a grudging smile.

"Right-oh." So what if it got cold? He zapped everything twice anyway; he liked his food steaming. "Probably eats ice cream hot," Maggie muttered.

"What?"

She started as he came up behind her in the dining alcove, trotting out her perkiest *Ozzie and Harriet* voice. "Welcome home, honey. How was your day?"

He slid into the booth—and her new routine. "Well, I'd tell you, dearest, but I had the strangest feeling you were hovering right there during most of it. How was yours?"

"Just dandy."

"I see you spent the afternoon slaving over another wonderful dinner." He folded down the table while she retrieved the warm dishes where they hovered in the air.

"Making the peas and carrots stay in their little compartments isn't easy."

"Don't complain. We used to eat Salisbury steak from tubes. Called it Salisbury toothpaste."

She shuddered at the thought. "At least this looks real."

"As American as TV dinners."

"And apple pie, which is our dessert."

His spoon stopped in mid-simulated-environment. "Real pie?"

She nodded, ponytail floating softly up behind her. "I made it before takeoff and found it in one of the food-storage containers this morning. You knew you were being restocked this trip, didn't you?"

"Nobody said apple pie. Although somebody ought to say thank you, shouldn't he?"

She smiled demurely at her plate. His compliment made her warmer than the coffee. "You're very welcome."

"Did I catch the words ice cream?"

"We brought it for your birthday, then promptly forgot it."

"All the excitement."

"Must have been." She anchored her napkin firmly between her knees, determined not to think of the exact cause of that excitement.

"Would you have a problem with me saying you'd make someone an excellent wife?"

She had problems every time that raspy voice dropped a notch and that smile widened.

"Not many women with half a dozen capitalized initials after their names would get excited by that," she said. Which didn't explain the thrill circling her heart like one of Saturn's rings. "It's hard to go wrong with no-fault, NASA-tested microwave meals."

"It was the thought, Maggie." He poked at the meat course. "Sorry if I insulted you."

"It's not that, it's just . . . I've never been much at womanly ways." Before she shrugged off any further compliments, she caught the gleam in his eye. "I'm serious."

"I know you think so."

"What does that mean?"

"You're about as womanly as anyone I've ever met. Decorating, cooking, putting up pictures."

"I taped one family photo to your dresser mirror."

"See? And you do that 'Honey, I'm home' bit to perfection."

She laughed. "If I know how to pamper boys and men, it's family background, not talent."

"Baking pies. Fluffing pillows. Crocheting that vest."

"You know perfectly well there are no pillows on board. And what vest?"

He didn't relish revealing how closely he paid attention to what she wore. "That vest thing you had on the other day. Handmade."

"Gran's handiwork. She'd be the first person to tell you how incompetent I am in the womanly arts."

He gave her a ruminative look. Maggie hoped it was a tough piece of steak. "Maybe I could convince you."

She sawed her own steak, unsure whether to expand on the theme or not. "You're wrong about me." Might as well say it out loud, she thought, she'd been saying it one way or another ever since he'd kissed her. She wasn't desirable, was hardly sexy, and certainly wasn't wife material. What most women came by naturally, she struggled for.

"When Gran cooks, she adds a touch of this, a dab of that. I stick to recipes as if they were instructions for nuclear weapons. I suppose jet pilots are extremely exact."

"When in doubt, go with your gut. It's called flying by the seat of your pants."

"And if you lack that kind of instinct?"

"Latch on to someone who has it."

"Mmm." She shied away from that idea. "Then we're complete opposites."

"Are we?" He stared openly at her now. So she thought she wasn't feminine. From what he'd seen, thoughtfulness, caring, and nurturing spelled woman. Mix in dashes of pride and vulnerability and the mixture got volatile.

Maggie was all woman and so loath to admit it, he could've plucked out her buffed nails and gotten no confession.

"You have a spot of something," she murmured. A drop of gravy clung to the corner of his mouth.

"Where?"

"There." She touched her own lip.

He licked the opposite corner of his.

"No. The other side."

Despite days of observation, he knew she rarely looked at him close up. He wondered what she saw and why it made her so skittish. "Get it for me, will you?" His voice was raspy.

Her fingers clutched her napkin. She reached across the table as if he might bite, and dabbed. "There. Good as new."

"Thanks." He left off the "darling."

"Anytime." She concentrated on her mashed potatoes.

He scraped the bottom of his dish. "You're not going to finish that?"

"Guess I expected better food on this cruise."

"At least you got to sit at the captain's table. We have shuffleboard on the foredeck, quoits on the aftdeck, and music on the tape deck. You have your choice between the best in country music and the best in country music. Maybe later we'll have dancing."

Oh no. She wasn't falling into that sweet trap. "To get back to our discussion of science—"

He'd gotten up to reheat the second half of his dinner. Bobbling a few kernels of steaming corn on to his spoon, he was more intrigued than ever at her change of subject. Science over womanhood.

"—your whole career has been devoted to furthering it."

"What is that?"

"The boundaries of science. Test-piloting, for instance."

"The whole premise of testing is that there's no substitute for manpower. People have to take a plane up, experience it themselves. Kind of like you and me up here. You have to live it, not look at it."

"Speaking of looking, I have something special for us tonight."

"Try me."

She swallowed the last of her coffee with a gulp. "It's a video I brought, one of my ideas about making this place homier. I want your opinion on it."

"Great. Bring your journal, and you can measure my pulse. Wouldn't be a *Playboy* video by any chance?" He watched her cast around for a suitably deflating reply. "Never mind. Hal sends those in plain brown wrappers. For those long nights alone."

He winked. Again.

"Maggie, what in heaven's name are you doing with those matches?"

"Lighting incense."

"Incense! When the atmosphere check kicks on, we'll light up every alert in Houston."

"I okayed it with Mission Control. Just enough to set the mood. Sit and tighten your seat belt."

Adam settled back on the sofa, literally strapping himself down. "This is supposed to remind me of Earth, right?"

"So's this." She smiled mysteriously as Adam grumbled.

She'd changed into a jumpsuit. It made her look slim and attractive. Adam had never been a hip man, and Maggie wasn't overly endowed in that area, so why was he staring . . . ?

Because he was horny, that's why. Sit still and behave, he told himself.

"Ready?"

He grunted. "Guinea pig A. Strade at your service."

She buckled herself in beside him and flipped on the remote. On the screen a roaring fire crackled and spit.

Adam sat completely still for thirty seconds. A minute. Two. "When do they roll the credits?"

"They don't. This is it."

"A fireplace."

"Yep. Homey. Comfortable. Warm."

It *was* warm in there. Adam convinced himself it wasn't his hormones or Maggie's perfume. Besides, that whiff of incense had driven out every other smell. "You didn't turn up the heat, did you?"

"Hal said no. Here." She pulled a light cotton blanket out from under the sofa cushion and laid it across their laps. "We'll sit here and watch the Earth go by." Her voice was almost a purr. "The fire flicker will crackle and we'll relax. Perfect after a long day at work, isn't it?"

"As long as the smoke detectors don't go off."

"Get into the spirit. The incense is olfactory stimulation."

"And the blanket?"

"Tactile stimulation."

"The fire's visual, I presume."

"And aural." She pointed the remote, increasing the sound of hissing wood. A log popped, and she jumped. "A good touch, huh?"

Adam put his arm around her shoulder. "Don't forget the human touch. Darlin'." He let the endearment stand. It seemed natural around her. The faintest shadings of pink warmed her cheeks.

"I didn't mean literal touches."

"What if I do?"

"We seem to waver between total formality and—"

"Kissing?"

"I was going to say friendship."

"Kissing's pretty friendly."

She turned to him, determined to disregard the fact her lips were less than a hand's width from his, ignoring that sweet smell of apple pie. "Kissing is outside the defined parameters of our relationship."

"What say we engage in some redefining?"

"We've set the limits."

"'Limits are for going beyond.' Page two of the manual. What did you expect with a man and woman sitting in front of a fire?"

"Camaraderie."

He laughed. "Come here, comrade."

She looked ready to argue, ready to tussle. A little wrestling could be fun, he thought.

"Adam, I don't think this is wise."

"Wisdom was the farthest thing from my mind."

"We're completely unsuited."

"I'm male; you're female. You know the guy who made that?" He pointed at the planet floating outside their window. "He made us this way for a reason."

His lips brushed her ear. "Remember, you're part of the experiment too. Give it a chance."

She had no place to put her hands. In her lap. On his thigh. One hand touched his arm as he squeezed her to him.

"Perfect after a long day at work," he murmured.

His lips tormented her ear, the lobe, the shell. A trace of dampness scalded her skin when fanned by his breath. She tingled like a rocket seconds before ignition.

She needed sense, not sensations. Intelligence, prudence—none of them qualities a man sought to arouse in a woman. She clung to them. "You're teasing. About the perfect day."

"If this ain't perfect, it's damn close. You like that?"

Yes. No! "I assume you've made your own informal study of what women like."

"You can't reduce this to a notepad."

If only she had hers! She'd squeeze it to her chest, except that reminded her how tender her breasts felt. She cleared her throat and tried for a deep breath. "I assume your studies were conducted in the field?"

"In fields. In cars. In bed."

"In cockpits?"

"Why do you think they call 'em—never mind." He chuckled low. "I won't touch that one. Besides, you saw the file."

"A space-age Lothario."

"I was."

"Before your marriage."

For a second he wondered how much of it she'd seen. "Uh-huh."

She pulled his hand down. It had strayed from her shoulder to her waist, her rib cage, the small swell of her breasts. "You were faithful to your wife, then," she declared.

"Can you get a little more personal? It's not as if we're strangers here."

"I'm sorry, I—"

"I said the words. It might sound old-fashioned, but when I take a vow, I keep it."

"I'm interrogating again. Sorry. I hoped we'd keep this more casual." She got her wish.

He withdrew his arm, hunching forward with his elbows on his knees. "You know, I think I've figured out the problem with your study."

That sounded uncomfortably like "You know what your problem is, lady?" Maggie had heard it all before. It wasn't easy, but she nodded for him to continue.

"This is too one-sided," he announced. "If you were to tell me a little more about you, I might feel less like Groucho and Fernando and more like a human being."

She couldn't completely agree with that conclusion. After all, Fernando's breathing didn't change when she swept her hair off her shoulder and resumed eye contact. Maggie had the teetering sensation Adam's did. "I have four brothers, but I told you that."

"Older? Younger? Bigger?"

"Definitely. We're a tall family."

"So I noticed. Are they big enough to beat me up if I get caught with their sister on the family sofa?"

"You're safe. They stopped intimidating my boyfriends years ago." They'd probably been too relieved when she managed to land one, she guessed. "Not that I meant you're—or that I'm—"

"Never mind, I got it. So you were the only girl?"

"After Mom died."

"Sorry."

"I was eleven. Dad saw to it I never became the little princess. I got into just as many scrapes as ever."

"Such as?"

"Burning down garages. Blowing up tree houses."

He looked duly impressed.

"Chemistry," she replied, as if that explained everything. "My nearest brother in age is now in the defense industry."

"Defending us from two-car garages no doubt."

"It wasn't attached. It didn't damage the house."

"Only a budding scientist's career."

"Marshall got blamed, so Dad insisted I accompany him on any future experiments. He didn't know I'd been tagging along anyway."

"A lifelong interest in science ensued."

"Everything this side of home economics."

"No woman's influence?"

Only a grandmother who believed a person learned best if relentlessly reminded of their failings, she wanted to say. "My father remarried eventually."

"Happily?"

"For all of us, yes."

"So you had a role model. That's nice."

"Yes." Except Laura seemed to think Maggie had picked up everything she'd needed to know from her own mom. That's when Maggie, insecure and gawky, had discovered that books held the answer to most questions.

The crackle of the radio made them both turn.

"I think your dad just turned on the porch light," Adam muttered. Unsnapping his seat belt, his voice carried to the console. "What is it, Hal?"

"Dad? It's me."

"Tad," Adam replied, moving quickly to the built-in screen. "How's it going, buddy?"

A shaky tenor sounded through the static. "Happy

belated birthday to you! Happy belated birthday to you!"

Adam cleared his throat and fiddled with some knobs, as if reception were the problem. "Enough, Sport. What're you doing in Houston?"

"They sprung me from the academy to come on down."

"Right in time for the hurricane."

Even from thousands of miles Maggie knew the boy understood his father's warning. His response didn't ease the creases in Adam's forehead. "I signed on for a training flight. Got to take the controls for a while."

"Through the outskirts of that storm?"

"Don't get mad, Dad; it was fun."

"Everything's fun to a nineteen-year-old," he muttered.

Maggie chuckled and put a hand on his shoulder. "Who's the babe—I mean, I forgot you had company."

"Ms. Mullins to you, Scout."

Maggie leaned over Adam's shoulder. "How're you doing"—she peered at the insignia on the young man's uniform—"Cadet Donnelly?"

"I'm fine, ma'am."

"Congratulations on your flight. When do you solo?"

"Not till graduation. You know, Dad was nineteen when he first took the controls."

"That was also during the tail end of Vietnam," Adam shot back. He'd been an older nineteen than he hoped Tad would ever be. "Besides, I had your father right beside me."

"I know."

"Aw, hell, way to go, kid. Sorry to rag on you."

"No prob. I mean, yes, sir. Gotta go; this is costing the taxpayers a bundle."

"Worth every minute."

"Happy birthday again."

"Tad?"

"Yeah?"

"You've turned into the man your dad wanted you to be. I'm sure he would've been proud."

The boy looked long and hard into the camera. "I hope you're proud, too, Dad." He said the last part loud and clear.

Clearer than Adam managed in reply. "If you don't fly out of there before twenty hundred hours Texas time, you're grounded until that storm clears, got that?"

"Yes, sir."

Adam saluted the image on the console before it blacked out. The silence was broken by the snap and crackle of a video fire. "Okay, let's get it over with," he said with a growl.

"What?" Maggie asked innocently.

"Did you arrange that?"

"What made you think—?"

"Because it sounds like something a woman would do, and it sure as hell wasn't Julie's idea."

Maggie stood her ground—floating a little bit up off the floor as he came closer. "A card isn't as nice as a call. As my gran said on every available holiday."

"Maggie?"

"Yes?" The chin went up.

"Thanks," he said. "Now get out of here so I can get some work done. I'm point man on that storm system, if you haven't noticed."

She couldn't have sworn his voice was huskier, or that that was a lump he kept trying to clear out of his throat. But she knew a bluff when she heard one.

Despite the fact it was a tricky move without gravity to hold herself at a respectable distance from him, Maggie laid her hands lightly on Adam's shoulders and pulled herself forward, giving him a very sisterly peck on the cheek. "Happy birthday again, Commander. We'll finish that pie tomorrow."

"Maggie?"

"Yes?" She turned, half floating out of the console room.

"Better put out that fire for the night."

For a second she wondered which fire, the one on the screen or the one smoldering in his eyes. She turned to the one that couldn't burn her and flicked it off.

Five

"I'm going to strap you down."

Maggie did as she was told. When Adam got bossy, the best thing to do was simply to obey, even when his hands were all over her.

"Ten days is the maximum for nonparticipation. I'm assigning you a daily dose of this."

"Yes, sir."

"How's your seat?"

"Fine."

"Move."

Maggie glumly pedaled the bike. Grigg insisted regular exercise prevented bone loss in space. Adam must have great bones, she thought.

"Don't you like exercise?"

"I like swimming."

"Same thing," Adam concluded.

"I don't see how a stationary bike—"

"Buoyancy. Zero gravity produces no drag, that's why the wheels are tension variable. Pretend you're going uphill or in a race. Where are you now?"

"In the welcoming bay."

"I meant where are you pedaling this thing?" He sounded exasperated.

"I'm running like a mouse in a wheel, isn't that enough?" She'd learned grousing from the master.

"Imagine you've in New England. It's leaf season. You're entering a tunnel of trees, reds and yellows and greens; there's a covered bridge up around the corner. You've got ten miles or forty-five minutes, so wherever you are, you'd better make it interesting."

Suddenly, an idea struck. Maggie twisted in the straps that held her to the saddle like some medieval torture device. "I have to write something down."

"It'll wait."

"I need my journal."

"Then stay there; I'll get it." He grabbed the spiral notebook that spun in Maggie's orbit as regularly as one of Jupiter's moons and gave it to her.

She let go of the handlebars, scribbling as she spoke. "Don't you see? A strong imagination is vital in space. One can augment mundane chores with daydreams."

"And all this time I thought they were just dirty fantasies."

Judging from his leer, those fantasies involved her. "Not if you were the last man on Earth, Strade."

"I'm the only man, and we're not on Earth. You know what I like?"

"Making me blush."

"Besides that."

"I'm sure you'll tell me."

Her journal rotated out of reach again, and Adam nudged it farther away as he wedged himself into a bulkhead to bolt his bike to the floor.

He mounted, the solid front wheel wheezing as he gathered speed. "You're getting testy. Maybe you should write that down too."

"You swatted my journal to the other side of the bay."

"Maybe it's the time of the month."

"Maybe it's your constant interrupting." Actually, she feared the two of them being so close, a combination as volatile as pure oxygen and an open flame.

"Want to know my favorite fantasy?" he persisted. "Adam and Eve."

When they shared a quiet moment in the evenings, gazing longingly at the planet Earth in all its innocence, Maggie could agree. But right now he was studying her openly, waiting for a reaction.

She jumped back into reality with both slippered feet. Sharing a fantasy with this man could be very dangerous indeed; better to keep him as anchored in reality as he was to that bike. "So this is Eden. And Hal's the snake?"

"He watches everything we do."

"Good thing to keep in mind," she cautioned.

"No cameras in here. A man needs his privacy. Another one of your mental comfort zones." He winked at her.

She stared straight ahead and pedaled. "Can't take the credit for that one."

"Why are you slowing down?"

Maggie grimaced but refused to pick up the pace. Her heart was hammering and her pulse was erratic. "I just found an imaginary hill. I'm coasting."

"Don't want to join me in my Eden, huh?"

If only he knew.

"It's a nice garden."

"Like Botany Bay?" she joked.

"I see us walking through it. The sun sets."

"As we hurtle toward the dark side of the planet."

"Stars come out. The moon shines on your skin."

"Cables snake through the undergrowth. Computer screens blink."

"You're not making this easy."

"Didn't know it was my job to."

A soft curse emanated from the man beside her. Maggie perspired freely now, vitally aware of his harsh breathing. She didn't need to glimpse him out of the corner of her eye to be aware of his body, a heady male odor.

Thanks to his quiet, persistent words, she smelled the garden, too, loamy and green, fertile. The ground would be mossy soft, damp with earthy secrets. She could almost hear the faint crackle as lovers lay down on leaves. . . .

"So you fantasize about us," she stated a little too loudly. "I'm sure that's healthy."

"Like sex?"

She blanched and felt the nubs of her breasts press tight to the fabric of the leotard she wore under her pantsuit. Sixty-eight degrees, she reminded herself firmly. And five miles to go. "That *can* be healthy, sure. In a mature relationship, when all factors have been taken into account."

"A man and woman who respect each other . . ." He groped for the words. "People have needs."

"Like regular exercise," she quipped.

"Keeps the body honed."

And the nerve ends humming.

"Good for morale too," he added.

You make it sound any less romantic, and I'll brain you with a wrench, Maggie thought dejectedly. *Needs! Morale!* "A purely physical relationship."

He didn't seem overly enthusiastic. "We could give it a thought."

"It wouldn't be sensible."

"Sensible isn't what I think about at night. Neither do you, Maggie."

"Oh no?" She positively prayed for sense as she lay cosseted in his hammock each night, dreaming of his arms surrounding her instead of down, of his lips tickling her ear instead of the cool metal prongs of a zipper. And night after night she searched vainly for sleep. No wonder her temper was short.

"Tell me your fantasy, Maggie." His voice was a low rumble over the whirl of the bicycle wheels. "Tell me."

"In my fantasy a prince appears to unchain me from this hellish contraption and slay the dragon who imprisoned me here. How's that?"

"I could play both parts."

"You'll have to. I don't think I could escape this setup if I tried."

"You should have thought about that before you signed on."

"How would I know you'd make me sweat—exercise," she amended hastily. "Anyway, that's not the setup I was referring to."

"What if Hal did set us up?"

"Then he is a snake."

Adam chuckled, a low and sexy vibrato. "You must have realized we'd be completely alone for days on end."

"Approximately forty days and nights. Downright biblical."

He laughed and sat up, stretching out his back, expanding his chest until the muscles were clearly defined against his khaki tank top.

The pulse-taking sensors in her handlebars beeped loudly. "Maybe I'd better slow down," she said, her breathlessness unfeigned.

"What are you thinking now?"

Maggie hated cutting him off when the man was so honest about his needs, so blunt about facing loneliness. But she had needs of her own. Self-preservation being high on the list.

I'm no good at this, Adam. Please leave me alone. She knew, as plainly and as purely as she knew the name of his aftershave, that she wouldn't subject herself to the kind of humiliating amateurishness that had wrecked her previous sexual encounters.

But he was right about one thing: They were absolutely, supremely, indisputably alone. Hal might clear his throat helpfully on the intercom before beaming up a message. He might find a sudden rash of chores for Adam to do in the evening. But Hal wasn't there. Maggie and Adam were.

Yes, she could be tempted into making love with Adam Strade. But she wanted it to be one hundred percent right when it happened. Not because a man of his experience would notice her errors, but because he deserved better, a better woman than she suspected Julie had been for him in eight years of marriage. A more spontaneous, earthy, natural woman than Maggie Mullins would ever be.

She wasn't the Eve for this Adam. And yet, the idea that he'd have to go on living in his garden alone made her ache with a sorrow that took her by surprise. She lowered her head, hoping he'd mistake two flinty tears for droplets of sweat.

That quickly he was touching her, tugging the straps loose, reaching beneath her arms to the buckle at her abdomen. He pressed it, releasing a series of sensations like tiny tremors deep inside her.

"My prince has come," she joked weakly.

"You slumped."

"I'm fine."

He called himself a few unflattering names. "I should have paid attention when that sensor buzzed." He didn't tell her to lean against him; he merely put one arm around her back and slid her from the confining belts.

She floated up, unsure where to go next.

"I gave you too much to handle your first time. Do twenty minutes tomorrow and work up."

Was that all? she thought morosely. "I will."

"Maggie." He tucked a finger beneath her chin, a concerned look furrowing his brow. "If I'm driving you too hard, tell me to take a hike. Understand?"

She nodded, for some unearthly reason feeling bewildered and lost. He wasn't the only one who needed to be needed, who felt alone in this cold, distant place, who sometimes longed for— "Adam?"

His eyes darkened; she didn't need to say more. He tilted her so she swayed parallel to him. He could have sworn her look meant . . . but what did he know about women? She was dizzy from overexertion after ten days of nothing more strenuous than bobbing. If he had any sense at all, he'd stop misinterpreting the breathless way she said his name.

"Hope you don't consider me the only bastard in the galaxy. A fella gets horny, well— You can tell me to take a hike for that too. It's just, with you and me, alone . . ."

"I know." His face was so close, his breath warm. She wriggled in his arms. "I'm the only woman for miles. It's understandable you'd turn to—"

"Maggie." He gripped the lapel of her pantsuit so hard, a Velcro pocket tore open with an ugly scritchy sound. Her eyes grew wide.

"There is no way on God's green Earth," he ground out, "that I'm going to let you believe I want you because I can't do any better. Got that? You're one hell of a sexy woman, and it's driving me nuts pretending otherwise."

"Yes, sir."

He still hadn't convinced her. *She* was the reason he wanted this contact, not hormones, not isolation. He wrapped his arms around her. "Kiss me, Maggie. Kiss me now or tell me to go to hell."

He didn't wait for her approval, or the denial that never came. Her lips parted. Unsteady and adrift, they were finally on the same plane.

"I thought you'd want to experience this too," he teased gently, his lips grazing her hair, his tongue seeking the faint recesses of her ear.

She tilted her head abruptly to the side, the sensation too intense. They tumbled, rolling in slow motion through the welcoming bay. He'd swept her off her feet, Maggie thought. A dangerous spot for two needy people with no one else to hold on to.

Her hands clung to his arms, climbed his shoulders, her palms tickled by the hair at the back of her neck.

"Keep doing that," he murmured, his mouth trailing over her shoulder.

"Does that feel good?"

"Oh, yeah. You believe me when I say you're the one who turns me on?"

She peered up at him and shyly shook her head no.

"But it excites you to hear me say it."

She nodded. His bluntness *was* stimulating. She peered at the deep crinkles framing his eyes and thought of him pointing a jet straight to the sun, staring it down. She wasn't that brave. She trembled because a man held her, his courage taunting her to give more. What would a man of his experience think of a woman of hers?

"If you want me, say the word."

The words were simple, yes or no. Adam read both in her eyes, along with caution, curiosity. She touched his face with the same look of wonder Eve must have shown when she encountered Adam for the first time. A man, so much larger, stronger, not half as gentle, but inside needing in all the same ways.

A surge of primal desire shook him. He was an explorer again, on the edge of discovering the uncharted territory of another human heart. He'd stumbled through the maze of his emotions for so long, maybe Maggie could show him the way out.

"Do you want me?" he asked. "I'm getting mixed messages."

Maggie laughed with a little huff. "The Hubble telescope sends clearer signals. I'm not sure what I want."

"Then say you don't want me."

"We shouldn't."

"That's not the same."

He kissed her ear again, then got greedy and slid his lips down the side of her throat in a slashing move that left her gasping. His hands splayed across the small of her back and pulled her close, intimately, unmistakably, man-and-woman close. "You're scared. Tell me why."

The direct order cleared her head for a moment. "You surprise me."

"How?"

"Men don't usually ask for words. They seek intimacy in physical expression."

He wondered what textbook she'd gotten that one from and ruthlessly concentrated on stringing kisses on her so-sensitive neck. "You want words, I'll give you words. Tell me what to say."

"And you'll say it?"

That slowed him down. He wasn't one to promise anything even if he knew what she needed. "I can only say what's true now."

"That you have needs."

He cursed the quotation. "That I want you so bad I ache with it. If you're by me I light up like a Roman candle, if you're not I wonder when you will be again. I wonder when we'll make love."

Maggie's head cleared completely. If only her lips would stop tingling, she'd be cured of this madness. "I hate to be a tease, but this has gone far enough."

"Afraid you'll get carried away?"

He'd already taken her to his castle in the stars. It was up to her to find her way back. "I'm afraid I'm not the kind of woman you're used to."

"And what kind is that?"

Willing. Spontaneous. Skillful. Words ricocheted through her head like asteroids. "It's probably been quite a while since your last encounter," she stated cautiously. "There was the marriage and that probably went bad a couple years before the divorce."

"If it was ever good," he muttered.

"So it's been a while for you. I can understand—"

"Hey, I haven't been a monk. There were some women on the rebound." His caustic tone was aimed less at her than at his battered pride. After the divorce he'd gotten what he wanted where it didn't matter, fast, impersonal, too wary to let any woman get closer than the other side of the bed.

Her analysis made him damned uncomfortable. He felt he was on trial for the crime of getting hot around a beautiful woman. "I haven't jumped any other women astronauts, if that's what you're wondering."

She unconsciously folded her arms, tugging up the zipper of her pantsuit as she moved out of his reach. "So it's been a full year for you . . . alone, I mean."

"Without sex, you mean. How long has it been for you?"

The words hovered in midair like they did, the antiseptic atmosphere charged with static.

"I've been in astronaut training for months."

"No one in all that time? Those boys pride themselves on their way with a joy stick."

"Yes, well. I'm used to being surrounded by brothers; we got along fine."

"On your terms."

"On mine."

"What if I don't want to be your big brother?"

"Adam, please, take my word for it, you're not missing much."

"Let me be the judge of that."

Her laugh carried across the bay; the smile stayed behind. "Spare me having to say 'I told you so.' Please?"

"What about your study?" Adam leaned against one of the exercycles, his foot resting on a raised pedal in a stance similar to Marlon Brando's in *The Wild Ones*.

"What does my study have to do with anything?"

He grinned a sassy, let's-kiss-and-make-up grin. "Don't you want to know what sex in space is like? One of these coed crews is going to run into the problem eventually."

"And it'll be just that, a problem."

"As a part-time psychologist, shouldn't you be concerned with the emotional ramifications of lovers in close proximity?"

As a woman, she couldn't help being aware of the

possibilities, right down to her toes. And the dangers. "So we should sleep together and check out our reactions, is that your proposition?"

"Make an interesting monograph."

She laughed out loud at that. "You are a devil, Adam Strade."

"Kind of fits the Eden motif, don't you think?"

"I thought you hated the idea of me analyzing you. You wouldn't want your, uh, performance presented on paper."

A bark of laughter echoed through the room. "I can't picture you describing that kiss we just shared, much less— Lose something?"

"Uh, yes."

He moved in slowly, decisively. "Maybe it was your fear of me. Was that it, Maggie?"

His nearness swamped any thoughts as mundane as finding her journal. His kiss damn near sunk the boat.

He lifted her with the lightest of touches, leaving her without a leg to stand on and no need to.

Her chin thumped the hard line of his jaw; her leg bumped between his. She found it impossible to suppress a moan as her mouth opened for his. His hand cupped her cheek, her neck, his fingers drawing the zipper down once more. His hand crept inside like a thief, a pickpocket stealing breath and doubt and caution, playing over the mound of her breast in triumph.

He drew the edges of her suit open and down, laying it lightly around her wrists, her waist. He sank down, tasting the flesh exposed beyond the outlines of a skintight tank top, the projection of a budded nipple, the bareness of an arm.

Every quivering inch of her responded to him. Her mouth longed for the taste of his, her fingers probed the taut muscles of his shoulders. When he bent to kiss her breast, her head followed him down, her lips pausing over the prickly hair at the back of his neck, razored short.

His lips, sucking gently through her shirt, shook her so profoundly, she groaned. It was as if the entire ship had been set adrift, they'd been marooned, the only two people in the universe.

She stroked his hair as tenderly as a mother would. Suddenly, she raked her teeth down the side of his neck—like a woman—and got the ramrod reaction she knew would come.

It was a test, pushing the limits of her own daring. Experimenting, experiencing, she listened to her heartbeat, the jumbled pulse. Was this what it felt like when you did it right? Was this the way? she wondered.

If she raised her arms, stripped these clothes, would his lips on her breast send her over the edge? She could try. She wanted so much to try. . . .

A voice from the past startled her, a man's disappointment undimmed. *"You mean you didn't climax? We could try it again."*

No, it's all right.

"I'll try something else."

"No, it's all right." Her voice caught, the words hollow and loud in the bay.

"Is it?" Adam breathed harshly. "Say you want me, Maggie. Say it."

She did. She had. But it was already gone. "Stop, please. Stop."

"I have, in case you hadn't noticed." Only a blind, insensate man could misread fingers clutching his arms, legs clamped shut, and a jaw so clenched, he practically heard her teeth grind. Her face was averted, her chin down, ineffectually protecting her sensitive throat. Maybe that was it; her breasts were sensitive, and he'd been mauling—

No. The woman in his arms responded like a firecracker, but Maggie herself was in another star system, a million miles away and still running. "You were with me a minute ago."

The accusation sounded so familiar, she flinched. *Why didn't you make it? You were almost there.*

"I lost interest," she replied coolly.

An expletive escaped him like a hiss of steam.

Just look him in the eye and lie, Maggie ordered herself. "I thought better of it, okay? I told you I didn't want to tease you."

"So it's my fault I'm left in this condition."

"There is a cure."

"Don't I know it. Every night for the last week—"

"I'd rather not hear about your nocturnal habits. However, I hope you keep this experience in mind." As humiliating, crushing, and mortifying as it was. "Think of it the next time you want to kiss like that again."

"Which one of us needs the shrink?" Adam muttered as he watched her leave. He had a split personality on board. The woman was near, then far; caring, then distant; apparently involved in everything he felt but this, this pounding, throbbing remnant of what it meant to be a man.

"Like kissing your sister," he muttered. Maybe that was it. She wanted to be a sister to him, and he wanted the woman.

"Hal, you got a lot to answer for, sending her here."

Adam puttered around the welcoming bay, dismantling the second bike. A French crew was scheduled to dock in four days; they'd need room to disembark.

Adam grabbed his shirt on the way out, scooping up Maggie's notebook where it hovered over the door. If only he could leave his worries behind as easily as she had her journal.

Adam went looking for the solitude he'd relished before Maggie had arrived.

The niche that served as his office consisted of a comic calendar from Tad, a corkboard littered with Post-it notes, a computer console, and a porthole facing Earth. He'd been happily working away, granting Maggie's wish of forgetting she was even around, when he realized she'd designed the space specifically for that purpose. How could he forget her when she permeated everything around him with her ideas, the small perfect touches he'd never noticed until he met the person who'd put them there.

She wanted him to forget she was a woman. "That'll be a cold day in Cape Canaveral, honey."

The woman was driving him. Not nuts, not even up the walls where she hovered so effortlessly. Just driving him.

What scared her? What motivated her? What did she scribble in that journal day in and day out?

He clutched it in his fingers, the pages ruled in red and blue, sections tabbed Personal Experience, Subject Observations, Conclusions.

The Subject went looking for answers.

And stopped when he got to the part about their first kiss.

Six

Propelled by blasts of air, water droplets pelted Maggie's body, rinsing away everything from salty perspiration to the tingling memory of Adam's mouth on her skin.

She closed her eyes and silently thanked the NASA engineers who'd mastered the tricky art of getting water to flow downward in space; they'd improved the quality of life tremendously. A cold shower restored a woman to her senses—or saved her from them.

Wrapping a towel around herself, Maggie glided from the bathroom, determined to write down this correlation. She got no further than the threshold.

Adam stood in the center of the room, her journal clutched in his hand. "Thought I'd give this back."

"Thank you. I was just looking for it."

Studying her kiss-swollen lips, his eyes narrowed as he speculated on what she'd planned to report this time. "I wondered if you left it as a test, to see if I'd read it."

"Thank you for not—"

"I flunked."

He almost heard the gulp when she swallowed.

Lifting that delicate chin of hers, she stared him in

the eye. "I would have expected otherwise from a man who values his privacy so highly."

"Would you?" He tossed the journal in the direction of the desk. No satisfying slap resounded as it twirled aimlessly, like a Frisbee unable to land. "How was I to know you didn't leave it on purpose? You've calculated everything else. Your April Fool's joke, Tad's call, my office."

"Designing situations to observe how people interact with their environment is part of my profession."

He withheld a terse opinion of her profession.

At first, flipping past pages of diagrams and calculations, he'd concluded she wasn't there to analyze him after all—too many sketches of their quarters, console-to-chair-height ratios, video glare, and so on. There were some personal notes, of course. With amused detachment he'd scanned her initial description of him as a porcupine.

Right now he felt as ornery and dangerous as one, every quill erect. "And our first kiss? Did I react properly to that, Maggie?"

Her description had barely done it justice:

Unaccustomed as I am to the physical fluctuations of space, Commander Strade's kiss (a light contact of the lips with minimal penetration of the tongue) had an uncommonly thorough effect upon my sensual responses. This need not become part of my report but will be noted for my own future reference.

He'd read it three times, pitiful as it was. Now he wanted her version of it, out loud. Let that luscious tense mouth lie to him in person.

"You know I never intended to kiss you," she whispered.

"Which leaves the question of when you decided to make it part of your study. Was it before you opened your mouth, Maggie, or after?"

She snatched the journal from the air and slammed it into a drawer. "There's an intercom in here. I'd appreciate not broadcasting this to Houston."

He slid the bedroom door shut, flipping the intercom switch to Receive only. "It's off. And we're just turning on."

Hauling her against him was easy. With no gravity, no foothold, there was no way to oppose him. His hands were warm as they framed her face; his eyes bored into hers.

Maggie knew he wouldn't hurt her, just as surely as she knew he'd kiss her. The advance warning proved a flimsy defense. A fuse had been lit in the welcoming bay, stoking the frustration building in them both. Anger, under the right circumstances, was as potent an aphrodisiac as loneliness, as potent as the kisses of a desperate, hungry man.

Primitive, deep, and scouring, his kiss lashed at her walls, tugged at her senses. He gave her no chance to step back and observe, no time to question her reactions, to weigh the prudent against the passionate. No time and no will to do anything but surrender.

"Open, Maggie. Open for me."

Maybe it was the grating rasp of taut vocal cords and tightly held emotions that made every nerve ending in her body respond in kind. Maybe it was the call of her own desires, too long unheeded, too long unmet, that urged her lips to part.

When they did, he claimed them with a moan of triumph, his arms wrapping her in a fury of motion, her own reaching, rising, twining around his neck. "Adam, please."

Her towel dislodged, slinking silently through the air like a genie's magic carpet. Shock rocketed through her as her naked body brushed against him. A slope of leg grazed his slacks; skin powdered dry surrounded a core of honeyed moistness as his hands swept her waist. A ruff of coiled hair nudged the juncture of his thighs, whispering against the unmistakable evidence of his need.

He withdrew his mouth, then his grip. For agonizing seconds nothing touched her but his gaze—which was everywhere. Her hastily folded arms couldn't conceal breasts pebbled with desire, an abdomen scattered with peach fuzz and freckles, a thatch of pale fire farther down. He took it all in, blatantly inspecting every inch before languidly making his way back up, his gaze coming to rest on her lips.

"Describe *that.*"

A moan caught in her throat. Whatever happened she couldn't let him see how deeply he'd affected her.

Summoning a semblance of injured pride, Maggie wiped her mouth with the back of her hand, slowly, undeniably. "I never calculate things like that."

The stinging truth of his retort pierced her as he turned to leave. "Baby, you just did."

At least now she knew what three days on a space station was like when the crew didn't get along! Maggie sighed, realized she'd been making a habit of it, and ran a hand over her hair. Name a cure for betrayed trust, she thought.

Adam had the idea he'd been her guinea pig. As if she exerted such control over her desires, she could tempt a man at will! Surely he'd seen through that by now.

But the journal painted another picture, letting Adam mistake the woman on paper for the one he'd held in his arms. Scientific, intellectual, analytical to the point of indifference, she was a woman in charge.

"Hardly." Maggie nibbled on a thumbnail. Yes, she thought too much, but that didn't stop a tiny, guilty corner of her soul from relishing the seething, unleashed passion of that kiss. She'd never been so instantly, electrifyingly, aroused. Or so quickly dashed. He might as well have tossed her back in the cold shower.

Sitting in her room seventy-two hours later, her lips were still tender, her self-esteem zero, and her privacy so thoroughly violated, she wasn't sure she'd ever reestablish it.

For the last three days she and Adam had alternately sniped and fallen back like retreating armies. They coolly drifted past each other in hallways, neatly avoiding contact.

For his part, Adam luxuriated in being able to work the lab alone, like the good old days. He puttered with the plants on top-deck, commiserated with the mice, and ate his dinner standing up, hovering over the console as if every blip counted.

As if Maggie Mullins were already gone.

Down the hall Maggie drove a laminated chopstick through the topknot she'd wound her hair into. She had her arguments ready.

The atmosphere on a space station was a closed system, the oxygen constantly recycled. Once poisoned it would stay that way unless something purified the system. Like an apology. "We're going to clear the air."

Cornering him on the bridge, she delivered her air-system speech along with a carefully crafted apology. "We can act like professionals," she concluded. "I'll melt into walls, I promise."

"The only thing you melt into is me when I kiss you."

She shuddered imperceptibly as he looked her up and down. The clothes she'd piled on could have been so much wet linen, transparent at that.

"You want to go unnoticed, Maggie? Can't bear another month of this? Go back to Earth with the French. Observe me via satellite."

"There are things I need to experience in person."

His suggestive smile taunted her. "I can name a couple."

"Don't you dare."

"What's the matter? Wouldn't a few succinct Anglo-Saxon words fit in that journal of yours? I can even tell you how to spell them."

She uttered a sample under her breath.

"I think you got the hang of it, Red."

A voice interrupted. "McAuliffe, come in, Space Station McAuliffe. Mind catching us up? I think we came in in the middle."

Maggie blushed at Hal's dry sarcasm. "We're having a discussion," she declared before Adam could offer otherwise.

"I take it the transmitter's working again," Adam said.

"Great job, Adam. You two didn't need to raise your voices at all."

Maggie covered her face with her hands. "They heard every word." She groaned. "See what you've done?"

"Fact of the matter is, Hal, we've got a personality clash. The observer is getting in the way of the observed. Order her down. Her job here is done."

"We'll take it under advisement, Commander."

"You do that. And while you're at it, let me know how my commission for Mars is coming."

Adam had come out of eight years with Julie knowing one thing only, he would never understand women. Never. Maggie's attempts at explaining this relationship from her point of view had him flummoxed. If that's how women thought their way through kisses, he was more ignorant than he ever dreamed.

He ran a hand through the thatch of hair tumbling across his forehead. Hal was waiting, and Hal was still the boss. "When will the French be here?" Adam asked.

"In the nick of time, apparently."

He swung around, glaring at the overhead camera.

Hal wiped a smile off his face with his customary silk handkerchief. "ETA oh-eight-hundred hours tomorrow, if the weather's good. You'll give final permission to dock."

"Do they have room for a passenger?" Adam said with a growl.

Maggie gripped the edge of the control panel, watching Hal's barely discernible reaction.

"Do you have any idea how many francs it costs to transport an astronaut, Commander?"

"Take it out of my pay. I can't spend it on the way to Mars."

"Ms. Mullins, do you have any supply requests?"

"Yes, I do."

Adam gave her a wide berth at the microphone.

When she was finished reciting her list, Maggie breathed a sigh of relief. Hal had signed off with no further comments on her return to Earth. She had four days to convince Adam to let her stay.

Like settlers spotting a Wells Fargo wagon, Adam and Maggie welcomed the French with open arms. They greeted new supplies and new faces with all the eager gratitude of shipwrecked sailors.

Two members of the science team took up residence in the space lab, the other two in the botany lab. Only Captain LeRoi remained on the bridge, singing under his breath in a passable imitation of Maurice Chevalier.

Adam sat at the table and scanned a copy of the latest issue of *Downtown Girl* magazine. Maggie's guest column advising teenage girls on science careers completely captured his interest. In between such questions as "Can you wear makeup in space?" and "How do you wash your hair?" he caught glimpses of the woman he knew.

Yes, she wore makeup, skillfully, subtly, rarely

enough to cover the freckles, usually enough to bring out the green and gold of her eyes. Her hair? It glowed soft and fresh each day, smelling faintly of peach.

Damn. How had he learned so much about her in such a short time? How could he ever forget her when these desires refused to go away?

As if conjured by his thoughts, she entered. Adam's jaw clenched, and he dropped his gaze to the brightly colored graphics surrounding her article. "Afternoon."

"Afternoon," she replied civilly.

Captain LeRoi turned from his data base and beamed. "Ah, Mademoiselle Mullins." He pronounced it "Muh-lawns."

She gave him a wide, unselfconscious smile.

Adam hated him already.

"Welcome back to the bridge."

"Thanks. Nice to see you again." It had been all of twenty minutes. She'd gone to observe how the other four divided up working space in the labs and had stayed to take notes. She gripped the journal to her side.

"This is yours," Adam said, tossing her the magazine in slow motion. She reached out and snared it. "Good shot."

She realized he was referring to the photo accompanying her article and shrugged it off. "Oh, that. A promotional thing for NASA."

"And a boost for young girls interested in science. You're becoming a role model."

"Like the woman this station was named for. It's a special privilege, and a responsibility. I want to tell them what it's like."

"I noticed the 'To be continued.'"

"I'll be filing a story this week. I've been working on it."

His eyes strayed to the journal. "What's that one

on? Dating tips in outer space? How to kiss and tell?"

Her voice dropped to a hoarse whisper. "You're not making this easy."

"Didn't know it was my job to."

She slid into a seat opposite him. *Fasten your seat belts,* she thought grimly, *it's going to be a bumpy orbit.* "Can we please lay this to rest? You know I'd never publish those observations. I was thinking through my feelings on paper. That's how I do it."

"Wanna hear how I do it?" He grunted. "What kind of woman has to explain kissing?"

"My kind." She dearly wished she could get up and pace. But LeRoi was at the console, and there were few places to find privacy with the station suddenly full. She had put their encounter off, hoping the company would ease the tension. No such luck.

She glanced at LeRoi's back. "A man can't think in French and eavesdrop in English, can he?"

Adam cracked a smile, the first he'd managed in days. He leaned over and flipped on the tape deck. "Don't mind a little music, do you, Pierre?"

"Not at all. I love country and western."

"*Merci.*" Adam turned it up a bit. "Keep your voice low and shoot."

Maggie folded her hands on the table, going over her explanation in her head one more time. "One of my theories is that people in tight quarters need to be particularly honest and open with each other."

"I don't care about your theories."

"Right." She twined her fingers and started over. "Unfortunately, I tend to confuse thinking with feeling."

"I'll say."

"You make me feel things I don't know how to deal with—so I try to think them out, reduce them to terms I understand."

"Like 'minimal penetration of the tongue'?"

Adam's grim smile produced a dimple in his left

cheek. For a moment Maggie wished she'd seized the opportunity to kiss that dimple when she'd had the chance. The words she was about to say would put a stop to any kissing. There'd be no more journal writing, so long as he gave her nothing to write about.

"Please listen until I'm finished; this is hard enough."

Adam leaned back, shoving his hands in the side-slash pockets of his slacks, crossing one ankle over the other as his heels hovered inches off the floor. With a nod he signaled her to go on.

Maggie fingered the smooth surface of the table. "I'm better at thinking than feeling. People tend to stick with what they're comfortable with."

Adam Strade exceeded her comfort level every time he scanned her with that unreadable look.

"So what makes you uncomfortable?"

"Answering questions such as yours." She laughed. "Getting into emotions."

"Getting physical?"

The blush said it all. So did the spunk that lifted her shoulders while she firmly returned his stare.

"I'm not very good at what you'd expect a woman to be good at when she kisses . . . oh hell, Adam, I'm no good at sex."

The console blinked ten times for each slow, doubtful blink Adam cast her way. Phrases like "You gotta be kidding" sounded in his head. But the painfully deliberate description of their kiss, her eager reaction to same, the skittishness when the heat got too hot, all reinforced her words. "Maggie—"

"*Excusez-moi*, Commander, could you perhaps give me the frequency ranges again?" Fifteen feet away LeRoi smiled obligingly. As he slowly twisted in midair the red and white cables linking his lap-top computer to the station mainframe lashed him to the console like Ahab to the whale.

"Sure thing," Adam said, spotting the difficulty

immediately. Clapping him on the shoulder, Adam spun the French commander out of his web, ran off a string of incomprehensible numbers, then pointed to the headphones. "Our gabbing might interfere less if you tried those."

Despite the real danger of being strangled by yet another cable, LeRoi donned the extra gear. "I will. Thank you."

"*Gracias.*" Adam sat down across from Maggie. "You were saying?"

"I think you remember."

"Quite a statement."

She shrugged, her hands flattening on the magazine. She thumbed the pages of her journal, turning down the corners.

Adam deplored the practice. However, the wisdom of loaning her books wasn't his immediate concern. Unless, he thought, the book was *The Joy of Sex*.

"I'm fairly hopeless at most womanly things. Cooking, cleaning, cooing over babies."

"Is that what makes a woman?"

"It's probably all tied together."

With cotton-candy string, Adam thought. But Maggie took the bonds seriously. "So what makes you think you're not good at—?"

"I've been told—by someone in a position to know."

His black expression revealed what he thought of a man who'd tell a woman that. "Did you kick him in the nuts?"

Maggie gulped down a laugh. "I'm trying to be serious."

"So am I."

She fidgeted, sipping hot coffee, wishing briefly it was in a cup and she could stare over the rim at him, eyes cloudy with desire and rising steam, sultry, vampish, utterly without a clue. "They call it spectatoring, watching yourself perform. 'Is this right?' 'Am I there yet?' Of course that gets in the way."

"Takes all the fun out of it."

Her small smile matched his. "I don't want to put you through that kind of fiasco."

"We might get past it."

"Trust me. It's even worse if we're *both* watching what I'm doing."

"A man who knows what he's doing might make a difference," Adam offered.

"I know the basics; it's the ultimate, the legendary orgasm I never seem to reach."

"Maggie." He stretched across the table and gripped her hand, staring deeply into her eyes. "*I'm* legendary."

After a stunned second she burst out laughing. Then she struck her forehead with the heel of her hand. "How could I forget! Even *Time* magazine says so!"

Adam chuckled and decided they could talk just as well while touching. He kneaded her palm with his thumb. "I don't feel like a failure if a woman doesn't light up like a pinball machine. Every time is different. And every woman."

Maggie knew what he was trying to say: "I won't pressure you." She recoiled at the memory those words evoked.

"What is it?"

"I've been with someone who said he didn't care either way. Unfortunately, it was true." She hated that catch in her voice.

He hated the man who'd put it there. "We're not all selfish bastards."

"No. There was just one."

The last one, Adam figured. And none since. "So I don't have a chance."

She shrugged, as if trying hard not to care. "I'm afraid to find out. No one's keen on humiliating themselves in bed. Kind of dents the old self-esteem."

He laughed and squeezed her hand.

Maggie glanced up.

"Funny how we go from barely talking to the most intimate conversations."

"Must be the intimacy of the living arrangements."

"Must be. You started by asking about my marriage."

"You needed someone to talk to."

"So do you."

"I doubt hearing about my sex life is very interesting. Hope I didn't bore you."

Bore him? He'd learned a bookful.

"I hope you see why we can't, or shouldn't, try again."

"Yeah, sure." He didn't mean a syllable of it, so he smiled and extended his hand. "Let's shake on it."

He wrapped her palm in his, reluctantly conceding he'd have to let it go soon. Try again? You bet he would. He had four days to cure her of this notion she lacked talent as a woman and a lover.

A nagging voice warned him she wasn't his problem to solve. She was scaring him off, not inviting him in. If he approached her like another "I can fix this" sheet-pilot, he'd lose her for good.

Strade, you're the last man in the galaxy to fathom a woman's problems. But hadn't Julie said there was one, and only one, thing he knew how to do?

Besides, he was the man Maggie had turned to. That swelled his pride, soothed his ego, and kicked his protective instincts into overdrive. It was his duty to do what he could.

He realized he was caressing her palm with his thumb when she pulled it free. "Time to fix dinner."

"They brought their own. Believe it or not, one of their crew doubles as a chef."

"You're kidding!"

Adam shrugged expansively. He loved the way her eyes twinkled when she smiled. "They're French, what can I say?"

"Huh! My hopelessness as a cook will be exposed once again."

Rising, he laced an arm around her shoulders as if he were an old friend. "I've been completely satisfied with your culinary efforts."

"Efforts is the word." She breathed easier when he touched her. A small part of her reveling in it, storing it away like a curio in one of her Velcro pockets, a memory to retrieve when she was alone once again. "Adam? With the new crew on board, I'll be observing all of you, how you divide up space, work around each other. I'll be taking notes."

He nodded solemnly. "Write all you want. Sorry I bent the grass."

"You what?"

"That's what pilots say when they come in too fast for a landing. I'm sorry I rushed you, Maggie. I didn't know."

She shrugged. *"C'est la vie."*

"Is that divine *français* I hear?"

"Lieutenant Charmain."

"Mademoiselle." The dark-haired science officer swayed to a stop, bumping his body alongside hers. *"Excusez-moi."* Bending over her hand, he brushed his lips across her knuckles with a Continental flair.

Adam's gut contracted. The woman was as off-limits as if he'd pointed her out on the orientation tour and said "Don't touch." He'd have to make that clear to this Gallic Galahad.

Then he'd find a way to make Maggie Mullins smile at *him* the way she was at the Frenchman.

Strade, it's not your duty to help every woman who claims she needs you.

There was the hitch. Maggie Mullins claimed she didn't, couldn't, and wouldn't need him.

His military training was as clear as spit-shined boots: Never volunteer.

His personal code of honor dictated he help a woman in need.

His hormones demanded one more taste.

And his gut said he'd regret it. So did his mind and what was left of his heart. By then he knew he was hooked.

She'd been looking for pencil-and-paper answers to flesh-and-blood questions. A woman needed a man for that. Maggie needed him to show her how.

It was physical, he insisted. He could keep his heart out of it.

Seven

"The French are garrulous, argumentative, instantly charming when a woman enters the room," Maggie recorded in her journal. "As if it's their national duty to flirt." She kept a smile to herself as the French crew gestured heatedly, twirling like tops as their enthusiastic hand motions spun them around in space.

Their attentions to Maggie had been sweet. Not for one minute did they forget she was a woman. For two days she'd been delighted, enchanted, and exceedingly well fed. She clicked more lead into her pencil. *A woman with this crew would soon feel she was either a distraction or a sex object, or both.*

No wonder the word *chauvinist* came from the French. She grinned.

"Impossible!" someone shouted.

The word needed no translation. Maggie had been busily reacquainting herself with the language, observing the newcomers, and reassessing Adam Strade. He welcomed a foreign crew as easily as an American one. She was the only one he treated differently.

That had been her intention after all. Too bad

discouraging Adam's reactions to her hadn't muffled hers to him.

When she realized she'd been staring at the same blank page for five minutes, Maggie closed the journal and sighed. "Guess I've come to the end of that chapter."

On the mid-deck bridge Adam switched off the camera to the science lab and went to work on the computer. What was he going to do with her? Two days had passed, and his determination to show her she was alluring and feminine had been bogged down under a French invasion intent on doing the same.

LeRoi, Charmain, Henri, and Cesare ardently seized the task of complimenting Maggie on everything from her hair to her complexion to her woolly socks. At first she'd been flustered by their attention, then shyly thrilled. On rare occasions Adam swore she even entertained the idea they might be right.

Adam punched a couple more numbers into the computer and let it chew on those awhile, acutely aware of the irony of his situation. He was the observer now, watching Maggie watch the French while they watched her.

He had to get her alone, had to make her see what every other man on board saw—Maggie Mullins was beautiful, desirable, and loving. But only he knew she was too stubborn to admit it, too hurt to try again, and too vulnerable to risk anyone getting closer than the pages of her journal.

Except Adam. Her secret honored him with an intimacy he planned to repay. But how? And when? "Confound it, Strade, now you've gotta make her stay."

"The mushrooms, they are not as fresh as usual. At home I would have picked them from the forest."

"They're wonderful," Maggie said, closing her eyes while savoring the red wine sauce.

Every man at the table licked his lips as she did hers, swallowing in unison.

Adam felt like throwing up. "Mind letting the lady eat in peace?" His teeth clamped down on a piece of sirloin tip.

"How do you enjoy microwave cooking, Henri?" Maggie asked.

"Well, mademoiselle, it is not easy without the flame. For dessert I could have made you a flambé of the most—"

"Are you nuts?" Adam barked. "An open flame on board?"

Maggie snatched her fork from where it bobbled in midair. "Commander, he only means—"

"Yeah, yeah. It's only talk." Adam stared directly at Maggie. "There's been a lot of that going around."

They sat in stony silence until Maggie exclaimed over the next course. Henri positively glowed.

Adam stalked to the pantry to reheat his soup.

Maggie sidled up beside him as he punched buttons on the microwave. "Maybe it wouldn't hurt to let it cool down a bit," she suggested lightly. "I may not be an expert, but I know harmless flirtation when I see it."

"That man wants nothing more than a handful of onions and the butter to brown them in."

"And what do you want?" If she'd known the question was going to slip out, she'd have looked elsewhere when he answered, when his eyes grew dark, his features set.

"I think you know what I want."

There was no mistaking the hunger. Maggie's heart sank. Her explanation had been useless; he still saw her as the one thing she wasn't. And he wanted her.

"Mademoiselle," LeRoi called from the table. "Please lend us your expertise."

"And your captivating presence," Charmain added.

"I'd better go," she replied unsteadily. She maneuvered toward the table, glad her shaking knees couldn't betray her in space. Adam wasn't a lonely stray; he was a man. What a cruel twist of fate that she couldn't be the woman he needed.

"We were discussing how civilized it is to have a woman on board," the captain remarked.

"Funny. I was thinking just the opposite."

"Mais non."

"It makes all the difference."

"Vive la différence."

Adam grunted and slid a box of steaming coffee toward Maggie.

Her eyes opened wide at the first sip. "If you have the right mix of men—"

"But women."

"They should be required on each mission."

"Indeed!" LeRoi slapped the table with the flat of his hand and bounded upward, saved from hitting the ceiling by the table trapping his knees. His comrades pulled him back down. "Anything else is uncivilized."

"College dormitories have experimented with this," Maggie pointed out. "Instead of segregating the sexes, some alternate male and female rooms. There's less rowdyism among the boys and less giggliness among the girls. It's more normal. Once everyone settles down."

Adam grunted as his straw hit the bottom of the coffee box with a slurp.

Charmain winced and smoothed back his patent-leather hair. "Nothing is more normal, or civilized, than men and women together. We French understand this. But tell us more about your work," he cooed, capturing her fingertips in his. "How one lives is as important as with whom."

Whom? For a moment Adam wondered if they had a class at the Sorbonne, *Seduction 101*.

Maggie chatted about her plans for the station. "We can't paint up here, of course, not with the closed atmosphere."

"It *does* get awful thick in here," Adam put in.

"And a little tiresome," Maggie quipped. If she didn't know better, she'd almost suspect he was jealous. "I plan on redoing the commander's quarters."

"That's where she spends most of her time lately," Adam added pointedly.

Charmain's brows lifted. Under Adam's icy stare the lieutenant released Maggie's hand and sat back meditatively.

LeRoi suggested a diplomatic interpretation. "You wish to make the commander comfortable. He is a lucky man."

Maggie blushed, as much from anger as embarrassment. "That's my job," she insisted.

"But of course." Charmain wasn't giving up. "You must come to our quarters also. You will tell us what we can do with our ship."

"I'll tell you exactly what you can do with your ship."

"Adam!"

All heads turned at Maggie's sharp tone. She flushed and offered them a belated smile. "Perhaps it's time I cleared the dishes."

"You've done it for three weeks," Adam declared. "With me. I think it's time we went back to the official formula. Charmain, you load the washer."

Charmain nodded, cordially aware of who was in charge. "Enchanted."

The next morning, hands splayed against the wall as if she were being frisked, Maggie arched a look over her shoulder as Adam entered the bedroom, her fanny jutting provocatively in his direction.

"May I ask what you're doing?" He lodged one foot against the doorjamb, pressing his shoulder against the opposite side in a deceptively earth-ly stance.

"Wallpapering."

He mouthed the word.

Maggie laughed at the scowl on his face. He'd been as ornery as a cornered skunk for three days now. "Do you always get tense when you have guests?"

"Somebody has to fight them off with a stick. Thought you'd appreciate the help."

"I'm an expert at discouraging men." She laughed ruefully.

"Is that why you wore that heavy sweater yesterday?"

"How very observant. Actually, they brought me this wallpaper, and I thought it was very obliging of them."

"They're an obliging bunch."

"They appreciate style."

"So do I." He grunted. *If it's yours.* Edging into a bedroom littered with redecorating paraphernalia, Adam felt bulky and gawky and gauche. A French word, that. He was picking up a lot of them. *Charmant. Délicieuse. Merde.*

"Hope it didn't bother you," he said, "my crack last night about you spending a lot of time in my quarters."

"I have."

"They might think—"

"Exactly what you meant them to think. But there's nothing to it. Is there?" She patted him on the arm and unwrapped a two-foot square of wallpaper for his opinion. "I've decided the colors are all wrong in here. I want to leave this room more cheerful when I'm gone."

Impossible, Adam thought with a pang.

"This blue makes the room seem larger, but it's too

cool. At first I thought you needed an aura of space, but . . ." She looked deep into his eyes.

His heart slammed against his rib cage. She smelled of perfume, lavender talc. Feminine and soft and elusive.

"What I think you really need, Adam—"

"Yes?" His pulse thumped.

"—are browns."

"Browns."

"Cozy and warm. Like a study or a den."

A long breath streamed out of him. "And at the end of the day I turn on my video fireplace and my video dog comes and lies at my feet."

She huffed, holding her sample to the wall. "Sometimes I don't think you take me seriously."

Seriously enough to want to change her life, Adam thought, and soberly enough he feared she'd change his if he insisted on pursuing this crazy idea. But what else could he do? The woman was intent on making a home for a man she believed couldn't love her back. "Maggie."

"Red and orange are warm, exciting colors."

He scanned her hair. She'd get no argument there. "What about hazel?" he asked. "Or gold?"

"For a bedroom?"

"Bedroom eyes. Hazel and gold are very attractive in a woman's eyes." He moved in closer. With a tip of his head he got her to tilt her chin as she unconsciously imitated his movement. "Hazel is a forest, cool and inviting. Gold is priceless, worth fighting for." He hoped that didn't sound like one of Henri's lines. Suave was something else he wasn't.

Maggie backed up, her hands searching frantically behind her for the wall. She didn't want her rear end bumping it and propelling her right into Adam's arms.

His voice was husky and compelling in the narrow room. "You're the expert. You tell me."

If only she could remember what she was supposed

to be an expert on. "Wallpapering!" She picked up the nearest roll and shoved it at him. "You've got to help me."

"I intend to."

She swung around, staring at a wall inches from her nose. "There's one thing I can't figure."

"Try me."

"How do I get it straight? The paper, I mean. A plumb line's no good without gravity."

"Does it matter? We're hardly ever right side up."

We. She refused to think about the way their bodies had swayed and rolled when they'd clung to each other. "It will have a subconscious effect, believe me."

"You should know."

She slapped up the first sheet of paper, inching and hitching it as her body revolved in reaction. Every time she pressed an air bubble out, she pushed herself away from the wall.

"I think it's me. I can't back up enough to see things right." The words hung in the air like the paste bucket she'd tethered to the desk, the brush she'd attached to it with a clamp.

Bustling around Adam, over him, everywhere but through him, Maggie tried to get a lead on whether the first sheet was straight. Not according to the edge of the mirror, it wasn't.

"I know!" She snapped her paste-coated fingers. How had she made such a mess of this in such a short time? "I could write an article on wallpapering without gravity. Think *Downtown Girl* would buy it?"

"Great. But first let's do this right. I hold you and no arguing."

The project went faster with Adam holding on to the porthole, corralling Maggie's body between his arms and the wall. Unable to avoid bumping him at every turn, she resorted to nonstop chatter, living up to the nickname her brothers had bestowed—Magpie.

She'd be pert, determined, and as enthusiastic as the first day she tumbled through the welcoming bay. Or so she planned until the image of another afternoon wavered lazily through her veins, the two of them gyrating in their own erotic dance.

Blood was supposed to thin at high altitudes, she thought. Why was hers so suddenly thick? Her body grazed his again. "Uh, Adam, do you have to do that?"

The low growl of his voice sounded close to her ear. "My mission is to assist all crew members in their tasks as needed."

"Does that mean rubbing up against me?"

Yes, yes, and yes. It did him no good to keep his mouth firmly shut; she read it in his eyes as she turned her head.

"Stand back and tell me how it looks," she ordered.

Adam obeyed, intently studying the patch on her jeans. "Looks wonderful from here."

"Does it?"

"Never seen better."

She clamped a hand to her backside and whirled around. "These are for dirty work."

He leered. "I can think of some—"

"Oh no, you don't! Heavens, one extra-large sweatshirt and a pair of ratty jeans, and you act as if I'm Marilyn Monroe."

"Ever notice your initials are the same? MMM?"

She waved him off with the paste brush. "You and the French, I swear that's all you think about."

He quickly drew the line between him and every other man on board. None had kissed her the way he had, held her the way he had, loved her the way he intended. "I've been wanting to apologize for that kiss, Maggie, the one in here."

"Good Lord, there've been so many you have to specify *which*!"

He moved up behind her, almost spanning her waist with his hands. "At first I thought those journal entries were about me. They're about you."

"Correct. I was analyzing my feelings, not your kisses. Glad we cleared that up."

"But there's still the kiss." His words were hushed, the admission for her alone. "I don't usually grab women out of anger. Scaring you is unforgivable."

Scared? Try unspeakably thrilled, Maggie thought, wondering what he'd think if she told him how her body had reacted. She hadn't believed it herself at first. Left abruptly alone, her first reaction had been to write it down, define the intense emotions rocketing through her.

But writing was hopeless. He'd branded her body his, and she'd handed him her soul on paper. He knew everything. She'd felt so naked, retrieving the towel had seemed pointless.

"I lived through it, Adam, no bruises, nothing broken. I understood, really I did." She put a hand on his arm. "We don't have to go over this again."

"Mademoiselle Mullins, this is so lovely!" Charmain fluttered in the doorway. "Such a change."

And when did you ever see her bedroom, Bud? Adam bit back the retort and glowered at the lieutenant.

"This paper we brought, she is satisfactory?"

"She's absolutely wonderful," Adam grated out. What did he have to do, post a sign? Off limits?

Charmain was charmingly oblivious. "You promised to come see our ship. You will not mind, Commander? We only have a few days with this beautiful lady, you have had weeks."

Translation: *If you blew it, that's your problem.* Adam knew more French than he thought. "The lady and I were busy."

"Is that so?" Charmain turned a pair of big, brown, puppy dog eyes Maggie's way.

"I'd be happy to take a look," she said.

Adam backed Charmain into the hall. "She'll be with you in a minute." He slid the door shut between them. It did irritate him. In fact, he was ready to chew nails. "You're not really going to their ship."

"I offered to give them some tips on how to enlarge spaces optically with color, and so on."

"It's the 'and so on' I'm worried about."

"Adam! You're acting ridiculous." He was acting jealous, but Maggie didn't want to put this in such personal terms.

"I don't want you alone on their ship."

"The last time I checked, my brothers were named Albert, Martin, Jonas, and Marshall." Maggie braced her arms across her sweatshirt. Too bad she couldn't tell him he was the only man present who made her heart tumble.

"What if Charmain tries something?"

Actually, Henri already had, but Maggie wasn't about to mention it. After Adam Strade's, deflecting another man's passes was a breeze.

Besides, it had been a rather halfhearted pass. Somehow they'd all gotten the idea she was sweet on Adam. Maggie was at a total loss as to how those signals went out. But as the saying went, when it came to love, how could four Frenchmen be wrong?

Who had said anything about love? she wondered.

Maggie hurried past him to open the door. "I have an appointment, and I believe you have other crew members to assist."

"You're not going unchaperoned."

Charmain bumped down from the ceiling, drifting debonairly between them as he took Maggie's arm and ushered her elegantly down the hall.

He smiled. "Did you know that *chaperon* is a French word?"

• • •

"I'm a little relieved," Maggie remarked dryly as they waved good-bye to the French crew.

Adam gave her remark a hearty endorsement. "Tired of 'em too?"

"I thought you'd send me back with them."

"For a while there, I thought you'd volunteer." It was safe for him to say so now that the French retro-rockets were firing his rivals toward their landing site in the Mediterranean Sea.

Space Station McAuliffe cruised around the edge of the Earth into night. Maggie blinked at the marvelous sight. Ninety minutes, and it'd be day again. How many ninety-minute nights had she spent with Adam? How many more in the next three weeks? She ached for him to touch her again, and ran when she thought she read the intention in his face.

She couldn't handle humiliating herself by getting into bed with him, but it was so hard offering friendship when love kept whispering in her ear.

He was a wonderful man. *Too wonderful for you.*

Self-protectiveness or no, she could no more shut herself off from a man who needed her than she could stand by holding a life preserver while someone flailed in the water. Adam was two hundred miles from shore, and she was there to give him something to hold on to—as long as she kept her own head above water.

She pressed her fingertips to the ceiling, and her feet briefly touched ground again.

Adam watched her reflection in the large window, the stars appearing on the far side of the evening Earth.

"Beautiful," he whispered.

"The stars, yes."

"Every time I look, I see something new."

For a few moments they watched each other's reflection, the air growing thick.

"Space Station McAuliffe?"

Adam punched the button. "Yeah, Houston."

"I have a communiqué here from the French government presenting their gratitude and thanks for this first in Franco-American cooperation, et cetera, et cetera."

"Thanks, Hal."

"We enjoyed having them." Maggie leaned across Adam to the microphone. Her breast brushed his shoulder. They both froze.

"Due to their early arrival, you two have the rest of the evening unscheduled," Hal commented. "Enjoy. Oh, and Maggie, the crew gives very high marks to having a woman aboard. It added immeasurably to the ambience, they said."

"They would."

"We haven't heard your opinion, Adam."

"I can't begin to tell you what having a woman means to me," he answered wryly.

"Maggie?"

She took extra care leaning toward the mike this time. "I don't think he's decided yet, Hal. As for me, you know my opinion. Mixing the sexes adds immeasurable psychological benefits."

"And tortures," Adam muttered under his breath.

Hal put extra emphasis on the next piece of information. "You've got three weeks and no more visitors. The Germans canceled with technical troubles. Next time you see a new face, Adam, it'll be your replacement, Max Crandall. If you two don't mind, we'll shut down transmission for the evening."

"Affirmative," Adam said, signing off.

The screen went blank. The red light on the cameras reduced to a pink glow. Adam threw some switches and punched in a couple of codes. "All alone," he said softly.

"Yep." Something uncurled slowly in the area of Maggie's solar plexus. Considering the hammering of her pulse, it was gratifying to know she still knew where her solar plexus was.

"No interruptions. No big brothers watching."

"Very true." A two-word sentence. Her mind and her mouth worked. Her legs did nothing but waver back and forth, treading water. A rivulet of anticipation rolled through her.

As if Adam were the moon and she the sea, an undertow pulled her to him as he turned, closing in silently. "What's for dinner?"

The better to eat you with, she thought nonsensically. "French leftovers and a movie they left us as a going-away gift."

"Let's go for it."

After dinner Maggie bustled through the dining alcove, transforming it into an entertainment center. The table was lifted and the back booth turned into a sofa, seat belts at the ready. She zapped some microwave popcorn and took her seat, the remote control hovering nearby. "I take it we'll have to keep this bag closed, or the popcorn will float all over."

"Unholy mess. I spilled one once. Picked kernels out of the air for days."

Maggie laughed and Adam cracked a smile, slumping beside her on the sofa, shamelessly stealing a handful before she could roll the bag shut again.

"Watch it, that's still steaming."

A mouthful of popcorn garbled his reply.

"What was that?"

"For a woman with brothers, you can be awfully dainty."

His compliment went over like a failed soufflé.

This was his big chance. The lady was relaxed, the radio was dead, and an evening of light entertainment awaited them. The night—well, they'd get to that.

"At least you don't sit around in a T-shirt and shorts," she retorted as the FBI warning scrolled across the television screen.

"Would if I could."

"Not around me."

"Around you, babe, I'd wear even less." He draped a heavy arm around her shoulders and tugged her as close as the seat belts would allow. "What say we neck until the movie starts?"

Eight

Maggie could barely focus on the screen, her eyelids drifting shut as he nuzzled her neck.

"What is this flick, anyway?"

"They said it was French." Her voice was as breathy as Bardot's.

"You gonna read me the subtitles?"

"Only if you stop teasing me."

He was dead serious, and they both knew it.

"If you don't watch, you'll miss everything," she insisted.

Everything was in his arms.

The screen went dark. He'd lowered the lights, the only illumination the glow of a thousand stars.

Adam nibbled her earlobe. Maggie hiccuped a little gasp, then let out a moan that impressed even Adam. He wasn't *that* good. Glancing at her dismayed expression, he followed her horror-stricken gaze to the screen

"*Last Tango in Paris,*" they read in unison.

Adam grinned from ear to ear. "Should be fun."

"Henri said it was a political allegory, something about American imperialism and French colonialism."

"Right. And *Deep Throat* is about Watergate."

Maggie fumbled with her seat belt, digging the remote control out from under her thigh where she'd trapped it so it wouldn't float around. If only she could trap Adam's roving hands the same way. On second thought, she didn't want Adam's hands between her thighs either.

She hit the freeze button. "We could watch *Beverly Hills Cop* again."

"No way. I'm looking forward to you explaining the allegorical references." He winked.

"You've seen this before," she cried accusingly.

"Never. But I like Brando."

Maggie believed it. Both men were known for raw power over finesse, each holed away on an island all his own, as far from civilization as it was possible to get. "You're going to weigh a ton if you keep shoveling in that popcorn."

"Want some? Come and get it." He stretched his arm in the opposite direction. She'd have to lay across his lap to reach it.

"I haven't seen such adolescent behavior since my brothers lived at home."

"Relax," Adam cajoled. Smoothing back his hair, he stretched extravagantly, very deliberately snaking his arm along the back of the sofa.

Another teenage move Maggie had picked up in a house full of boys. Marshall and Jonas had even practiced it on her: "Aw, come on, Magpie, you play the girl."

But how? She certainly couldn't use the actress on the screen as a role model.

Adam huffed and rubbed a kink out of his shoulder. All that exercise to burn off frustration, and now he had to sit through this. "This was rated X in nineteen-seventy-whatever."

Her voice was unnaturally perky. "How bad can it be?"

Adam clamped the bag of popcorn over his lap, wondering what came next. "We could watch *Aliens*."

"I've seen it. In between my fingers while baby-sitting Marshall's eight-year-old."

"Me, too, but I wouldn't mind watching it again."

"I'm surprised space movies would appeal to someone who's actually been there."

"Yeah, well, I never had Sigourney Weaver on board running around in that T-shirt and bikini underwear."

Maggie laughed. "Too bad you don't now."

"Don't I?"

Maggie rolled her eyes. "Hal was right. You've been living alone too long."

"I've seen you in space suits, jumpsuits, jeans, and towels." She blushed. He grinned. "Everything but your lingerie."

She made the mistake of looking at him when he rolled the French word off his tongue.

Adam tasted a crystal of salt as it dissolved on the corner of his lip. His voice was dry and low, as intimate as the subject. "Ever picture me in my underwear?"

She knew those black briefs would come back to haunt her! Maggie stared fiercely at the screen, miserably failing to keep the red from her cheeks. "We'll watch this," she stated. *And I'll get through it if it kills me.*

They got through one hour. Maggie declined to sink into the inviting angle of Adam's shoulder and chest. With no gravity she could perch on the edge of the sofa until kingdom come.

The tousle-haired French actress wound her legs around Brando's waist. The man exuded sexuality; harsh, unrefined virility. But it was so much flickering tape compared to the man beside her. "He was a lot younger then," she remarked inanely.

"Unh," Adam said.

"She can't be very old."

Adam grunted.

Aware Adam might be teasing her with his Neanderthal replies, petrified that he might, in fact, be every bit as affected by the scene as she was, Maggie sat like a rock. An escaped kernel of popcorn floated within inches of her nose. She leaned forward to grab it in her mouth.

Something stopped her, a strand of her hair twisted around Adam's index finger.

He didn't apologize. Something told her he'd never apologize for wanting a woman. As with the other facts of life, he got to the point, zeroing in on the subject she'd been dreaming about since the movie started.

"Ever tempted to make love with a stranger?"

The question sent shivers down her spine. "No."

"We could pretend, Maggie. We meet for the first time, we're attracted, we're alone."

"No."

"Might be exciting. A man who knows nothing about your past. Someone you wouldn't have to make excuses to," he added softly.

When he put it like that, part of her flared like a flame. But Adam wasn't a stranger; thanks to her confession, he knew her too well. "If I tell a man what he can't expect, excuses need never be made."

"Because you'll never make love."

She nodded, and they sat through another scene, this one hotter and heavier than before.

"Care to explain this?" Adam asked impatiently, indicating the simulated lovemaking on the screen.

Her throat was as arid as the Sahara Desert below them. "I think that's imperialist domination."

"Is it." Adam reached around her, clasping the remote control to her thigh. He pressed the pause button. "What would you say to a little domination? Something that didn't give you time to think?"

Like his angry kiss, the one that had shaken her so deeply. "Adam."

He hauled her into his arms. "We're supposed to sit here like good boys and girls and *think* our way through this flick? I say just do it. No arguments, no words. Not even names, Maggie. Just you and me, a man and a woman."

"I say we watch the movie." Unyielding as plywood, she sat as stiff and as stark as the fear he'd put in her eyes.

Adam dropped his arms. "So much for the caveman routine."

"Maybe we should give this up altogether," she murmured, shaking fingertips readjusting her sweater.

"Just keep explaining it to me," he snapped. "You explain everything so well."

His snide remark stung. Maggie couldn't help it if she thought things through. People didn't couple and uncouple the way they did in the movies, with no emotion, no reverberations. No scorecard.

She'd been naked in his arms, raked by his gaze. Could watching a movie be that hard to handle? It was when, minutes later, he lifted her hair and gently pressed his lips to the back of her neck, whispering the word "Sorry."

Sensations assailed her like pirates storming a ship, waves crashing over the bow. If he ever guessed how much she wanted him, she'd be lost in those kisses, dragged overboard by swirling desires a movie couldn't duplicate.

His voice was all male and much too human. "I have excuses, too, Maggie. Eight years of hearing how little I knew about women. Hearing if I had any sense at all, I'd stay as far away from 'em as—"

"As Mars?" she offered, her voice softening as his grew harsh.

"Yeah." He dragged a fingertip across a string of pale freckles, raising goose bumps.

"Is that why you're going?"

He shook his head, a terse rebuttal. "That's why I came here."

"A Foreign Legion outpost."

"Mars is a different dream, Maggie. I could be the first man in history there. Like Magellan, Eriksson, Columbus, all the great explorers. A man doesn't pass up a dream like that."

And a woman? Maggie suddenly thought of a book she'd read as a girl, *Sacajawea*, about the Indian woman who'd guided Lewis and Clark. A man didn't have to go alone. "So you're going to Mars."

"With Hal's say-so."

She met his cautious gaze. "Hal wanted my opinion on how you were holding up. But I've never had the final say."

"And if you did?"

She shrugged. "I'd say you were doing as well as could be expected." For a man alone. "Of course, I'm not an expert."

His smile changed, the crinkles at the corners of his eyes deepening, his chest rising in a deep breath he exhaled slowly. "I don't need you to be," he replied quietly.

There it was again, the tug on her heart, like the moon drawing the tide in its net. The real moon hung outside their window, cratered with scars all its own, bathing them in milky light. No wonder her blood flowed like water.

"Mars," he muttered, looking at Maggie. The woman had a way of getting a man to reveal his dreams and his doubts, of giving support. She looked at him as if he was her hero, as if she'd give him everything, her life included, if only she knew how.

For once he wished he was as good at talking as doing. "Men can be wrong, especially when it comes to women." He should know. "If a woman doesn't . . . isn't . . . thinks she can't, well, it's as much the man's fault as hers and from how you've described the bozos you've slept with—"

Her gaze darted away, and she turned her face, unaware her hair was still tangled in his fingers.

"Ow."

He muttered a curt expletive. "I haven't pulled a girl's hair since third grade."

She laughed, unsnarling it. "Did it work?"

He gave a short bark of laughter. "Don't remember."

She studied him a moment, half coquette, half frightened doe, all red-haired siren.

"Okay, I do remember. Her name, her address, and the color of the dress she wore the day I snuck my first kiss."

"Age eight and you were kissing?"

"Seven. I skipped a grade. I was very precocious."

"I'll say!"

"It was only on the cheek."

"And you progressed rapidly from there."

"I'm not talking about sex, Maggie, I'm talking about—" What? Sense? Emotion? Love? "Those guys, you can't let them label you." Psychobabble, that's what he was talking!

He ran a hand over his face and wondered how long his skin would hold up under the regimen he'd adopted since the French arrived. Shave twice a day, slap on cologne, wash it off as too obvious, pat on some more, check his hair in the mirror. He hadn't been so self-conscious since he was sixteen. Who the hell was he to talk sense to a woman?

Especially one who had the presence of mind to look at him like a kindly older sister and pat him on the leg.

"I apply my own labels, thank you. I know what I can and can't do. I was being honest when I said I wasn't any good at sex. Some people just aren't—coordinated, uninhibited, something like that."

"So you read definitions of your problem in books."

"And watch demonstration tapes." She cocked a thumb toward the television screen.

Adam had to laugh, just as he had to run a hand across her hair, the texture and spring of it giving softly under his palm. "And what if you're wrong?

What if the only one you can't study is you? You can't get the distance."

"And you can? Is outer space far enough? What are your labels, Adam?" She held up a palm. "I've already talked to Hal. This is strictly between you and me."

"My labels." He poked around in the bag for the last of the popcorn, offered it to her, then crushed the bag into a ball in his rugged fist. He stared at the television. "Insensitive. Unfeeling. Selfish. Crude."

At the last word he shifted his eyes to the lighted crescent of the Earth between them and the moon.

"Those were Julie's labels, weren't they?" Maggie ventured.

Shoulders hunched, Adam listlessly tossed a bag he couldn't drop from one hand to the other. "She had a point. A man with a son to raise doesn't test jets. A man with responsibilities doesn't risk losing his life to earn a living."

"Did that apply to you or Todd?"

"You mean she was mad at Todd for dying, so she took it out on me."

An insensitive man wouldn't have insight like that, Maggie thought. "Could be."

"I knew the woman for ten years, Maggie. Or thought I did. Turns out the only thing I knew about women was how to get 'em in the sack. I knew blank-all about marriage."

Maggie smiled at his attempt not to swear. Crude? Hardly. Vigorous and virile, definitely. He was none of the names Julie had called him, none of the names he called himself. "Excuse the platitude, but no one can predict how a marriage will work out."

His dark eyes flashed as the sun sliced over the horizon behind him. "Then how can anyone get married?"

"Faith," Maggie said. "Love."

"Duty and promises aren't enough?"

"Your promise was to Todd, not Julie. You have to promise each other."

He took her hand in his, letting the bag drift away. "Women want promises. They deserve more than a tumble and a play-by-play of their performance."

She flinched, but he wasn't letting go. Somehow they'd ventured onto new ground. This was between them now.

"I want you, Maggie. If I can give a woman anything, that's it, a night you'll never forget. I could show you what you've missed. Let me do it for you."

The Earth shimmered just beyond him. Maggie found herself blinking back tears. "Adam."

Her fingers were clasped so tightly in his, she wasn't sure which of them held on tighter. His rough palm rubbed hers, pressing until nothing came between them.

"Honey, are you gonna believe them or you gonna believe me?"

"Do you still believe Julie? That sex is the only thing you have to offer?"

His stony gaze searched out the surface of the planet below as if his answer were etched in the dawn-lit mountain peaks. "If I can be sensitive with anyone, give to anyone, it'd be you. I can't think of a better way to show it."

Not by making promises. Maggie knew he couldn't share his future with her. He was destined to be a man apart, a hero traveling through a cold and vastly empty universe alone. And *he* wanted to help *her*? Selfish? Unfeeling? Not in a million light-years.

Maggie touched his face. "I'd die rather than disappoint you."

"Just try it."

The prod of his thumb undid her seat belt. He drew her legs across his lap, hugging her to him. His kiss was long and tender. Maggie returned it with all the blossoming love swelling her heart. For once, words failed her.

They failed him too. "You got the sweetest— derriere." He almost choked on the French. "Honey, you got the best behind this side of Jupiter. You mind me saying that?"

She shook her head, smiling, beaming, stroking his face as she touched his lips with her fingers. She had to find the words. None of the women he'd known had taken the time to tell him how much he meant to her, how good and strong he really was. "Kiss me again."

He obeyed. When she opened her mouth, he was there, this time plunging and taking like a pirate, balancing her body in his arms ready to carry her off to a swaying bed. "Just tell me what you want. It's your ride, Maggie."

The truth lodged like a stone in her tight throat. "I want to be better at this than I am."

"Then come with me." A stark command coupled with another unadorned, explicit kiss. He felt her heart hammering next to his and bridled his desire. A tender "trust me" kiss followed. The woman thought she couldn't do it right. He was out to prove her wrong.

To prove she had the sweetest skin, he tasted her cheek, the point of her chin. To prove her neck was swanlike, he trailed kisses along it, seeking her mouth again when his tongue went exploring, discovering with her the things that made her body sing.

And that was only the start.

He stroked her small, pert breasts, unzipped her jumpsuit and touched them, lifted her plain blue T-shirt and kissed them. She almost jumped out of his arms.

The first nipple was smooth, rosy, and conical. With one touch of dampness, one strafe of his teeth, it hardened to a tiny nib. It fit in his mouth, all of it. He was sorely tempted to take it that way, devour her like an animal and listen to her groan. But he wouldn't rush her, not this time.

He lifted her shirt on the other side. Her body arched effortlessly, weightlessly in his hands.

"I have a lace chemise," she whispered, grasping his head to her chest. "I could put that on."

"It's not the lace; it's the woman in it." The statement sounded pat, but he meant every word, electrified by each sound she made as he brazenly uncovered her other breast and treated it as tenderly as the first. "Do you believe me, Maggie?"

"Yes."

Trembling with sensation, she lolled her head back. Adam listened to her hair whisk the back of her suit, his hands trapped inside against her heated skin. "Let me pull this down." He drew the top half to her waist, the dry air of the cabin whispering over her skin.

"How far are we going?" she said with a gasp, aware she was half-naked in his arms.

"Only as far as you want to go, babe."

Maggie took a slow breath, trying to calm her racing pulse. It worked until he spoke again.

"To the moon and back again. To the stars."

"I don't know if I can."

"Once around the Earth then."

Ninety minutes. A night with Adam Strade. A lifetime. Didn't someone say "You only go around once"?

Movie dialogue mumbled in the background. A shot rang out. Their heads turned to catch Brando's last words, something about following the woman from Algeria to Indochina to Paris.

"I'll be damned," Adam said. "That *was* a political allegory. Maybe we'll watch it again tomorrow."

"Are we making a date?" She played with the insignia over his pocket, flicking it with the jagged edge of a chewed fingernail.

"I plan on seeing a lot more of you."

"You don't have much choice. I'm the only woman here."

"You're the only woman I want." He stood, holding her to him, letting her slide against his front, unashamed of the hard evidence of his desire or the curious exploration of her hands.

She tugged his shirt free of his elastic waistband, her fingertips cool and searing at once, flitting over his chest, each crisp hair uncurling and springing to life at her touch, triggering shooting stars of sensation deep inside him.

She moved down, tracing the soft indentations the elastic made on his skin, thumbing his navel when he sucked it in, roaming over his abdomen, and softly, so softly, delighting in her power to provoke.

He loved her laughing eyes.

And he hated with a passion the fool who'd promised to let her take her time.

But not half as much as the idiot who'd set those alarms. A bump jolted them, a thud from top deck, followed instantly by the shriek of alarm bells.

"What is that?"

"Something hit us!"

Maggie jerked away from him, her legs tangled in his. Scrambling to pull her T-shirt down, she wrestled with the arms of her jumpsuit.

Adam punched up the schematics for the top deck, turning on cameras one by one as he checked for damage. Maggie turned on the second bank, peering at pictures of eerily silent interiors, switching at last to the cameras mounted on the station's surface.

Adam cursed at what he saw, then hit a button and killed the alarms. Maggie's voice sounded metallic and overloud in the sudden silence. "Well?"

"Either it was an asteroid or space junk. I'm sealing off everything above level C. Got that? Those alarms ring at Mission Control too. When they come on line, they'll want to know what we did."

"And I'm supposed to tell them?"

"Yep. I'm going outside to check."

An hour later Adam wished he'd done more than

bark orders at her as he'd swung down to the welcoming bay for his space suit.

An hour later he wished he'd told her he loved her. But it was a crazy idea now. What good was the love of a dead man?

Going through the uncanny motions of a space walk, he'd slowly made his way over the surface of the ship. Above Botany Bay he scanned the clump of jagged metal wrapped around what was left of Solar Panel Six, like a hideous modern sculpture clinging to a flagpole.

In the blackness a serrated shard of metal silently detached itself. Swooping past him with deceptive speed, it neatly, almost fatally, severed the thin silver tether holding him to the ship. If he hadn't caught the last of the strut, it would've flung him off into the void.

Gripping the strut now, he calculated forty minutes of oxygen left and no way to get back to the welcoming bay door. One slip as he crawled over the ship's surface, and he'd be falling through the vacuum of space, praying his oxygen ran out fast rather than slow.

Praying he got out of radio range before Maggie heard him die.

Nine

He looked up. That's what people usually did when they prayed. On every side was blackness and winking pinpricks of light.

"Adam?" Maggie's voice crackled over the speaker embedded in his helmet.

"Yeah, babe."

"I've got Hal. Can you hear him?" She sounded scared.

To be honest, so was he. "Space junk ripped off Solar Panel Six," he reported. "When I came up here to check it out, a piece of it severed my lifeline."

Maggie gasped. Adam wished there were an easier way to say this.

"I'm holding on to what's left of the strut, but part of that junk is tangled around the top. My plan is to go up and knock it free before it comes loose and crashes into the panels of the botany lab." If the carefully contained oxygen rushed out, top deck would explode.

"One tear in your suit, Adam—" Hal said.

"Yeah, I know," he said, before Hal could go into detail. One tear in his suit, and the oxygen would escape his lungs in the same exploding rush. Bile rose in his throat. It was no time to panic.

"Just hold on," Maggie said, as if knowing instinctively what he needed to hear.

"I'm not going anywhere," he croaked out, happy to hear her voice.

"Damn you, Adam Strade, if this is some kind of practical joke, I'll kill you."

"If I survive this, you're welcome to try."

They both listened in as Hal and half a dozen NASA engineers discussed the possibilities. Yes, the space station was constructed of modules. Yes, the destruction of one wouldn't necessarily hurt the rest of the ship.

But if it did? Adam thought.

What about detaching top deck, someone suggested, jettisoning it for the sake of the station?

"You can't," Maggie insisted. "Adam's up there."

"If the deck blows, we could lose both of you," Hal retorted. "We have to think of the station first."

"Unless someone comes up with a better idea," Adam replied calmly, "I'm going up and detaching the debris."

"Not without a tether," Hal ordered. "One slip, and you'd be drifting through space."

Adam knew that as well as anyone; he just hadn't wanted Maggie to hear it. Staring at the abyss surrounding him, Adam listened to her choke back a cry. "Thanks a lot, Hal."

"Adam, tell me about the tether," Maggie softly commanded.

Her voice twisted something in his chest. He thanked the God of all this darkness that she couldn't watch what was happening. The only camera his side of the ship had been mounted on the destroyed panel. "The tether's attached to the welcoming bay door. I strung it out approximately ninety feet to get around to the top. That's when I got clipped."

"How much is still attached to you?"

"Maybe five feet."

Maggie closed her eyes as a cold shudder ran through her. That's how close the debris had come to hitting him. A frigid wave of fear passed, leaving an idea in its wake. She called up a schematic of the station, checking distances. If eighty-five feet of tether remained, she could follow it out and *almost* reach him.

Hovering anxiously at the main console, Maggie switched to the speaker for Mission Control. "Hal, what if I could reach him?"

"Let's see if he can reach you first. Since we assembled the station in modules, there should be seams everywhere. Can you get a handhold, Adam?"

"If I get a good push in the right direction, I could propel myself toward one." And if he missed . . .

"Don't you even try!" Maggie cried.

"Sorry, darling. Just a thought."

Hal cursed softly, an event so unprecedented, Adam's eyes widened in surprise.

"Why, Hal, didn't know you cared." He chuckled.

"I suggest you conserve your oxygen by saving the smart remarks."

As voices ricocheted between the satellite, the station, and Earth, Maggie's questions interrupted the static just often enough to keep Adam listening. He didn't need the hushed urgency or the bloodless language of Houston to tell him he was out on a limb.

Maggie and the station had to come first. When he put it that way, the answer was easy. "We've wasted enough time," he announced. "I'm going up and clearing the stuff off."

"Be careful."

"Be careful."

He lifted himself hand over hand up the strut, the movement laborious in the bulky suit.

For Maggie's sake he kept his breathing even and his voice smooth. "Don't you worry, babe. If anything happens to me, they'll have a shuttle up here in a couple days." Another handhold, another foot.

"You've met Max Crandall. He's the man they'll send to take you off the ship. There are supplies for two months, so even if weather delays them, you'll be okay. Hal will be on the line to you night and day if you need the company. God knows, he baby-sat me enough when he thought I was lonely. For a while I thought that's why he sent you."

"Hush up," Maggie said, tears choking her. "You're going to be fine."

"You're better than fine, doll. Don't let anyone tell you different." The debris teetered ominously just above him. "Looks like an asteroid got the better of someone's satellite and the wreckage hit us. I'm shoving it off now. Maggie, take cover."

Voices that had ricocheted through his helmet like rain on a tin roof fell silent.

"Done. It's floating clear of the station."

A cheer went up he could have heard from Houston itself. Adam took a shallow breath. It was a waiting game now with only one outcome—a man never outlasted his oxygen.

He squeezed his eyes shut and curled his fist around the strut. A woman shouldn't have to listen to that, not when they'd been so close to making love. "Aw, hell, Maggie, I'm sorry."

"Adam?"

He'd spoken aloud. He busied himself tying his short tether to the strut to hold him in case he slipped. "Sorry I ruined our evening."

That was either a laugh or a sob. She quickly regained control. "You don't think I'm letting you off that easy, Commander."

"You gonna come and get me?" He practically heard the light bulb click on over her head. "Hal, tell her she isn't trained."

"Every astronaut is trained for an emergency like this," Hal stated blandly. "Maggie, what do you think?"

"I'll need another tether."

"She's not doing a space walk! Besides, the other line's in storage; she'd never find it in time."

There was a clunk as Maggie grasped the mike. "There's eighty-five feet of tether. I could get within five feet of him."

"Not exactly," Adam interrupted. "I flew a ways before I caught this spar. There's gotta be ten to fifteen feet between me and the closest reach."

Silence. At least he had talked her out of risking her neck for his.

"We'll improvise like the test pilots do," she suddenly declared. "Seat-of-the-pants stuff."

On the bridge Hal's voice sounded from a separate speaker, one Adam wouldn't hear. "Maggie, he's not going to like seeing you there. He may refuse to reach for you if he fears pulling you off the ship."

"Then I'll reach for him. I'm going to the welcoming bay for my suit. Keep him busy till I get there."

Hugging the base of the strut, Adam was surprised at how quickly the voices died away. "No suggestions, Hal?"

"Conserve your oxygen."

To what purpose? The few minutes that would save would only give him more time to think and look down on the botany lab glowing green beneath him, a second Eden he'd never share with his Eve.

Light-headed, he swayed. His choice was stand there and die, or try to reach that seam. He estimated how hard he'd have to push off as he loosened what was left of the tether.

Before he went, there was one thing he had to say. Maggie had made such a difference in his life—he was sorry he hadn't made more of one in hers. "Maggie?"

"This is Hal. She's coming out."

"I told you no!"

"There's no other way, Adam."

In the welcoming bay Maggie flicked on the radio switch in her helmet as she struggled with the various clamps and attachments to her space suit. "Hal, can you hear me?"

"Read you, Maggie."

"I've got the atmosphere pack set and I'm clamping the helmet to the torso now. I'll be out the door in five minutes."

"Take it slow, Maggie. You'll find the end of the tether clipped to the hatch as it opens. Attach it and go to your right."

"Roger."

The helmet smelled like popcorn and plastic. Maggie had the curious sensation of watching her gloved finger push the depressurization switch. Oxygen drained from the bay. Waiting, she expected to be flooded with emotion: fear, anticipation, nerves. Instead she felt nothing but a rock-solid love and a clear-cut awareness of what she had to do. "One step at a time," she said.

The exit hatch slid open, revealing the void. The tether snaked through the empty atmosphere like a rope in a magician's act. She reeled it in and looped it through her belt. "Am attached."

"Affirmative, Maggie. Head right twenty meters, then climb up and over the left wing. You'll find handholds on this part of the ship."

"I'm on my way."

She crawled past the docking doors and over the giant painted letters USA. In minutes she peered over the curve of the hull where light glowed from the botany lab. There stood a single strut, and Adam holding fast.

His voice hissed in her ear. "Hal, I told you not to send her. Go back, Maggie. I'm going to jump for the seam."

"Wait for me." Unable to see his face through the reflecting visor of his helmet, she played out the tether until the last few feet cinched her waist. "Houston, I can't reach him from here. I'm untying the tether so I can hold it in one hand and reach with the other."

A chorus of "don'ts" rang in her ears, the loudest from Adam.

"Any other suggestions?" she asked tartly.

"You stay there and I'll push off," he ordered raggedly. "You catch me—"

"As you go whistling by into space? Not a chance."

He didn't like the idea either, not when she put it that way. The last thing he wanted was her watching him die. "You can't ask a mission specialist to risk this, Hal. Order her back, and I'll take my chances. If we both die, what happens to your precious ship?"

Two suited figures hovered ten feet apart as static joined the sound of their breathing. Finally Hal spoke. "Do as she says, Adam."

"Please," Maggie whispered. She'd been so cool in the welcoming bay. Now her palms ached and her knees trembled. He had to say yes.

She unwound the tether, retying it to her wrist.

"Boy Scouts tie better knots." Adam grunted.

"Not with these gloves on."

"You never told me you were sending Supergirl, Hal."

"Superwoman to you," Maggie snapped out, anger sparking through her. "Now reach for me!"

Five feet separated them. Adam tied his line to the strut, holding the last of it in his hand, then he stretched for her fingertips. "I'll have to let go."

"I'll catch you."

"If I come at you too fast, duck. Don't try anything dumb."

"I did that when I fell in love with you."

A wry grin crooked his mouth. "I love you, too, Maggie."

Her last broken plea sounded in the starlit darkness. "Then come to me."

The helmet prevented Maggie from instinctively lifting her hands to block her ears. There was no shutting out the cheers resounding over the radio as she and Adam tumbled into the welcoming bay and closed the exit hatch.

Their helmets smacked together as Adam danced her across the room and tried to kiss her. In ten minutes the atmosphere would be restored. Ten minutes, and they'd strip off the suits and really touch each other, smell each other, hold each other instead of padding and packs. She'd never wanted to touch anyone more.

"Margaret Mead Mullins, I'm recommending you for the highest civilian honor this country bestows."

"Thanks, Hal," she replied, not really listening. In the harsh white light, she could finally see Adam's face through the tinted visor. Her own love showed through just as clear.

She stroked her glove down an ugly tear in his suit, superficial but deadly if it had gone an inch deeper.

Closing her eyes, adrenaline coursed through her. When inches meant the difference between life and death, the few feet that had separated them out there became a chasm. Fear swept her with a shudder. "Oh, Adam."

Clumsily, he folded her in his arms. "Maggie. Babe."

"Cabin readings report atmosphere restored," Hal announced.

"Hal. I owe you a report first thing in the morning."

"Right, Adam. What about surface damage?"

Adam impatiently pulled off his helmet. "First thing in the morning," he repeated.

Hal got the message. "Unless we hear otherwise, we'll await your report. Adam? That's some woman you got there; hold on to her."

"As soon as I get off this mike I intend to."

The static died. They were alone and breathing. Maggie unfastened her own helmet. Exhaling with a whoosh, she shook her hair out over her shoulders.

They didn't kiss, not for a long moment.

"Need some help getting out of that suit?" he asked mildly.

She nodded very slowly. "The sooner the better."

Hands as steady as his voice, he unlocked the connections at her wrists and drew off her gloves. The sleeves came next, then the leg units. In the same order he'd undressed her the first time they'd met.

"I hate this suit," she said, drinking in his murmured reply. At last his was a real voice, undistorted by mikes or transmitters. His hands were competent and sure, his hair telltale slick, stuck to his forehead with dried sweat. She reached up and smoothed it back. "I hate anything that gets in the way of me touching you. Helmets, gloves, my own fears."

She brazenly unhooked the joinings of his suit. Her gaze met his, her hands stretching the knit fabric of his shirt in her haste to remove that too.

His chest expanded on a deep intake of breath. She had to say it, to tell him everything.

"The feeling of not being able to reach you, of never touching you again—" Her throat tightened painfully. She cleared it of tears. "I never want to be in that position again."

Adam hauled her to him. "I know. I know."

"Don't say it. Show me."

"You have any idea what that does to me, coming from you?" He cupped her behind and pressed her tight to him, running one hand over her waist, her breast, her throat.

She shuddered deep inside, a riot of emotions, from fear to relief to love and desire, sweeping over her.

"You're every man's fantasy. You gotta know that," he whispered, his lips skimming her hair.

Her cheek grazed the late-night roughness of his. "I don't want fantasy. Show me real, Adam. Please. I thought for a minute we'd never get the chance—"

He knew it, too, that sick dread of knowing you were too far out on the edge. The sicker recognition that someone you loved was watching, would hurt long after you were gone. In one flashing second he'd cared more about her than himself. The feeling hadn't faded. "You once said this reminded you of a waiting room at O'Hare. We can do better."

"Take me there."

"Now?"

"You could take me anywhere in the universe, I'd go."

She had come out and danced along the edge of it with him, shared the danger. It was only right they share the love.

"I love you," he said.

She nodded.

Sweeping her into his arms was easy without gravity. He said a lot of things, made a lot of promises. As they moved down the corridor he was suddenly the one who couldn't stop talking. "We'll live in a house, any kind of house, and we'll have kids, any kind, all kinds. You like kids?"

"I'd never planned—"

"How about horses? You want a ranch? Anything, Maggie, anything you want."

"Adam?" She ran her hand down the back of his head, inclining him toward her. "Shut up and kiss me."

He did. For about an hour. When they came up for air, her back was softly bumping the doorjamb. Her clothes were in disarray, his anatomy straining the fabric of his slacks.

"Our room," he said, with what was left of his voice.

She nodded. She wanted to please him, to make this perfect because she loved him. She wanted to be everything he'd ever needed in a woman. There was so much tenderness spilling out of him, so much gratitude. "I saved your life."

"Let me save yours."

Once inside, he didn't waste time shutting the door. There'd be no interruptions. Passion gripped him as the zipper grated down her jumpsuit. He watched his hands lift the T-shirt over her breasts, her upraised arms. The desire interrupted earlier by the alarms sprang instantly to life.

He stripped off his own shirt in one move, then, bracing his back to the wall, he slid her body up his. "Feel me." He buried his face in the corner of her neck, the cleft between her breasts. There'd be perfume at her core. He'd taste her, excite her; they'd rocket through the night together.

"We'll use the hammock," he said. It'd be like Earth, her first time making up for all the other times.

She mutely agreed, her hands tracing him, outlining the sleek ridge of him. "May I take these off?"

"Be my guest."

A faraway smile lifted her mouth at the sight of black cotton briefs. She played with the elastic around his waist until he thought he'd burst, toying with him until his teeth ground like stripped gears. "Maggie, if this is affecting you the way it's affecting me . . ."

Guiding his slacks down his hips was a whole different proposition when his anatomy caught on the edge. She sidled up to him, chest to chest, heartbeat to heartbeat, and slipped her hand inside the warm darkness, curling her fingers along the taut shaft, teasing skin that was smooth and quiveringly sensitive, hair dark and springy. He bucked in her grasp.

Clutching her wrists, he hauled her up, clamping one leg around the backs of hers. "Hold on."

"I was," she murmured.

He wanted to kiss the sultry smile right off her lips.

She pouted as if she'd read the rebuke in his eyes, a move that made him rethink every label he'd ever used on witchy women. "You know as much about lovemaking as any ten women, and don't ever let anyone tell you different."

For one giddy, towering moment she believed him. "You tell me." Maggie chuckled.

He left her no time for doubts. Skimming her nipples with the backs of his fingers, he felt her tremors reverberate up and down the seismic scale.

Each inch of him throbbed with expectation. He drew her hand away from danger and kissed her palm in a hungry male kiss, wet, erotic, and unsubtle. His softly voiced commands were gravel on velvet. "It was worth living to do this again."

And he'd done it a lot. The thought flashed through Maggie's mind. Girls, women, a wife. He'd wined and dined and flown them everywhere but to the moon. She stopped her train of thought. She wouldn't compare herself to women she'd never known.

Adam wouldn't either; he wasn't that kind of man. He cared, he caressed, so intent on pleasing her, she felt drunk with his attentions. *Let me please him*, she pleaded silently. He deserved more, more than she'd ever been able to give.

As if underwater, he lifted her easily by the waist and they bounded gently upward toward the hammock. He tucked her legs in the oversized sleeping bag, her knees bumping the air mattress inside. A stiff board inserted behind it simulated the earthly feeling of lying on one's back. Absolutely nothing could duplicate the sensation, frank and carnal, of having a naked man crowd in beside her, each rigid inch of him sliding down her skin until they were face to face, chest to chest, and thigh to thigh.

"Comfortable?"

"Yes," she replied as he eased their bodies around, the scent of his skin rich in the folds of the quilted material. She'd smelled him every night in this room, wrapped in his hammock, dreaming she'd be wrapped in his arms.

Dreams couldn't compare with reality any more than Maggie could compare with other women. *Stop it, Maggie. He wants you.*

"Because no one else is here," her conscience replied. "Because you saved his life. This is thank you, Maggie. This is a payback."

"Maggie?"

His voice brought her back, sounding in her ear, hot on her flesh. She got her arm free from the cocoon of the sleeping bag and stroked his cheek. "I'm here."

Was she? A smile quirked his lips. "If you're wondering about birth control, I've taken care of it." Maybe that's why he'd lost her for a minute.

"Oh. Thank you. That's certainly prudent."

"Babe, a word like prudent doesn't belong in the same sentence with what I plan to do to you."

Her eyes widened.

He chuckled, hoping she felt the movement all the way to her toes. "This'll be the greatest time you ever had sober. Promise."

He was teasing. She smiled, a demure smile that made his heart turn over. "Supergirl's become kind of shy here," he murmured, his lips on her skin.

"I don't think Supergirl ever got it on with . . . well, whoever."

"And Sigourney? If you'd come crawling across that top deck in your underwear, I couldn't have been happier to see you."

She laughed, mortified that it came out sounding like a giggle. "You've got the weirdest imagination."

"My fantasies never prepared me for a heroine like you." Although they'd prepared him a hundred times for this, when he'd fought for sleep knowing she was just down the hall. He kissed her hair, inhaling until the motion brought his abdomen in tighter contact with hers. "I ought to thank you."

Paybacks. Maggie wriggled beneath him. "You don't have to. I mean, if this is how—"

"Hush. This is how I tell you I was never gladder to see a woman in my life. Never happier to hold her in my arms. And never, never so alive. If you feel even a fraction of what I feel right now, Maggie, show me."

She felt it. An intimacy that surpassed any melding of bodies or limbs. They'd shared the edge, that hollow, scoured feeling of seeing someone you love in danger and the greed for sensation that followed so close on the heels of risk.

She'd reached out her hand. He'd made the leap. She wasn't letting go. "Adam, touch me again."

"Where?"

"Anywhere."

He did. His body was solid, crowded against hers, incomparably, undeniably real. Out there the void waited, empty, desolate, as lonely as death. Inside was life and love, longing surging through them like an electric current.

His chest pressed hers, the hair tantalizing her breasts. There wasn't much room, and when he reached around to zip the bag to their waists, there was even less. When he wedged a hand between them, her stomach rippled, vibrations fluttering deep inside her. She was coming undone.

She mewed, and he parted her thighs with his and pressed his swollen flesh to her sweet center.

"Wrap your legs around me, Maggie."

She did. He waited. He wanted her with him, unafraid, trusting. That meant caring about her needs, showing he did, and letting her show him how she felt in return. That meant putting it in words—if he'd learned anything from her journal, he knew Maggie needed words. "Do you like that?"

"Yes."

"Tell me what you like."

She hesitated.

"You like my size, Maggie?"

She swallowed and nodded. He caught the dip of her chin with his kisses and dotted her temple with more. That gave her access to his throat. She took it, her mouth tracing the broad line of his neck, the convulsive bob of his Adam's apple. Her lips sizzled along his beard.

"How does it feel?"he asked. "Tell me how I feel on your mouth."

"It makes my lips tingle."

"And the rest of you?"

She ached, another kind of hollow. She wanted to open for him, but something kept her tight. He pressed gently, relentlessly, up and in until she felt his shaft parting her, filling her to its length. Muscles she couldn't control shuddered convulsively, deeply, her body reacting to his invasion with searing sweetness.

His chest flexed against her as his arms tautened. He gripped the board at her back and pressed his body relentlessly to hers. "Am I heavy?"

"There is no heavy in space."

But he could simulate weight, simulate what a man felt like lying on a woman as she took him in. He withdrew and entered again, a sure, deep stroke. "Can you cross your ankles?"

She did, up around his waist, her saucy wiggle making him grind his teeth. His tip teased her, in and out as she maneuvered. If that made her half as crazy as him, they'd be there soon. He'd take the woman he loved on her first magic carpet ride, a mile-high club of precisely two members. "Maggie, anything you want. Put it in words, babe."

"Love me," she whispered, "love me."

Ten

He sank into her, a slow glide into a tight tunnel. He had to clench his teeth to speak and not moan. "That's it, babe. You're with me."

"Oh, Adam."

"Feel good?"

"Yes."

"If I do this?"

"Yes."

He wanted to wrap his arms around her and press her into the mattress. He wanted the experience to be just like on Earth yet different from any other experience she'd had. He'd loved other women, pleasured them. With Maggie he yearned to capture her every gasp and sigh, to prove how special she was, how great she could be.

Suddenly the idea of teaching her how and sending her away whole soured. Other men wouldn't hold her, love her. He'd flatten anyone who tried.

"Am I touching you right?" The other, younger Adam wouldn't have thought to ask.

"Yes. Please, go faster."

"Maggie." His voice was a harsh pant, his thrusts as deep as his sexy words were short.

Earthy sounds, pungent and incredibly arousing,

filled the cabin. Maggie clenched around him and felt a ripple like distant thunder. "Say that again."

He chuckled, swore at what the motion did to him, then shuddered inside her. "You like it like that."

"I like you."

His body rumbled with laughter, coexisting with the building rhythm of his passion. If this was *like,* wait'll she saw love. "Come with me, Maggie. Come on."

Her legs wrapped tighter, higher, her body open to his as to no one before. His erotic words were replaced with groans, guttural commands, his tongue a plunderer ravishing her unfinished cries.

Come with me, Maggie. She heard every word. Felt every move, each blessed rending plea. She was *too* aware. She was thinking, dammit, losing the sweet physical thread. She groaned, her head shaking back and forth on the pillow. "No, no, no."

"That's it, baby."

She couldn't risk disappointing him. With other men it was shame. With Adam, love. She loved him too much to let him know. He was so close to what she'd never had; she couldn't stop him now.

His buttocks clenched; her legs did too. She marveled at the control that let him withdraw to his very tip and quiver there. She clung, her fingernails indenting the skin of his back, slaking the ridges of his shoulder blades as he drove into her. She cried his name. He chanted hers. Beseeching, she begged him to continue.

But not with words. Words would choke her. She could wrap him in her arms and love him until the stars exploded around him in showers of sparks and his body spent itself inside her. She could treasure the sensations of pleasing him, spare him the frustration of knowing she didn't share them.

Then it was done, three quick shattering thrusts. He touched her gently, kissing her breasts softly as he withdrew, kissing everything but the tears sliding down her cheeks.

The fear all imposters knew gripped her. It would only be a matter of minutes before he asked.

He gave her room to breathe, easing to his side in the cramped hammock. "Are you comfortable?"

She nodded. A hole in the ground would be better; she needed a place to crawl.

"Here." He turned a little more, keeping one arm across her middle, as if, in this confining space, he still wanted her near him.

A sweet ache opened up in her. How could she not love the man? How could she dare lie about what had just happened? *Oh, Maggie, you fake.*

Seconds dragged by. Minutes. His breathing evened. A cowardly part of her hoped he'd fallen asleep. He hadn't.

Then, instead of asking how it was, he proceeded to mildly, seriously, tell her how it had been. She was magnificent. Stunning. He'd never loved a woman like her. He felt exhausted, rip-roaring, wrung out, and over the moon.

"Plowed." He grinned, running out of expressions. "Hope you don't feel exactly like that."

Cleft by a blade? Oh yes, she thought. Somewhere near her heart.

He kissed her hair, his fingers idly toying with the frizzy golden glow.

Dutiful and protective, he'd taken on the responsibility of answering for her. She was immensely relieved. And utterly furious. Instead of caring enough to find out, he acted as if he already knew.

But what would you have done if he'd asked? Her conscience chimed.

Lie, she answered.

Some heroine. Supergirl was a super fake. So good she'd fooled an experienced man like Adam Strade.

At least she'd learned one thing: In space, tears still rolled downward.

• • •

She wasn't asleep. Wasn't close. Adam felt the tiny shudders of a woman crying and ran out of silent curses long before he came up with any explanations.

Regaining his life and making love with Maggie Mullins packed quite a punch for one night. He'd gotten there fast and easy, convinced she'd been with him every step of the way. Hadn't she been?

He'd *listened*, dammit. He'd thought—

Which only proved he was as far from understanding women as ever.

How could he ever really know a woman? For a moment he'd thought Maggie was his answer. In a crisis she'd shown her true colors: courageous, daring. He'd trusted her with his life. What did Hal say before signing off? "That's some woman you got there; hold on to her."

Adam had tried, driving her until he'd thought they'd both go mad or go over the edge together.

She'd been so close, pieces of her had to be thrumming still. He could touch her, down there. Shock her with an intimate kiss that would spiral her straight to the stars. He could *make* it happen.

And he'd be just the same as every other man who'd tried to solve her problem. Orgasms weren't the issue. Self-image was. She thought she was less than a woman and only one lesson was going to teach her otherwise.

Few options presented themselves. Maybe simply lying there with her would prove she was desirable no matter what, that it didn't have to happen every time, much less the first time. Let her know he loved her anyway. "Maggie?"

She tensed. Here it comes, she thought, the Big Question.

"I love you."

She closed her eyes and bit down a cry. She

touched him in reply, a substitute for words she couldn't speak.

"You've saved my life in more ways than one," he said.

"Danger sometimes makes people want to reach out."

Adam scowled. "The danger made me admit it. I think I've loved you quite a while."

She patted his thigh. In the confines of the sleeping bag, he couldn't get his hand there quick enough to trap her against his flesh and show her exactly how much he felt for her. She slipped away.

"Whaddya think we were doing when those alarms rang?" he asked, voice clipped and hoarse. "You think I wasn't about to love you then?"

"Getting aroused by a dirty movie is customary."

"So you feel nothing for me." Adam hated himself the minute the words were out. In her hurt silence he remembered the tears.

He snaked an arm around her back and hugged her whether she wanted it or not. "Hold me, Maggie. Hate me if you want; I'm a clod and I ought to know it by now."

"You are not."

"Then what am I?"

"You're an incredibly brave, gallant, conscientious man and just too—" If she finished the sentence, she'd be as good as admitting she'd faked everything. "You're going to Mars," she said. "And in three weeks I'm going home. Can't we just leave it at that?"

Sure, he could leave it. But in his heart she'd go where he went, everything about her from her laughter to her caring to how he'd failed her. *Not on your life, Maggie Mullins. You're not getting away from me.*

He never did figure out how she'd slipped out of the bag without waking him. He found her in the dining alcove, the microwave pinging gaily as she zapped waffles. Adept at maneuvering without gravity, she neatly avoided meeting his gaze.

" 'Morning, Ozzie," she sang out.

" 'Morning, Harriet. Breakfast smells wonderful." But not as good as her hair. The syrup couldn't taste as sweet as her skin, and when it came to other places, honey had met its match. "Maggie?"

"Sit down, it'll get cold, and you'll be up ten times reheating it."

He wanted to reheat her, burn her breezy game-playing right off the video screen. Gripping her arms, he swung her around. His look said, "Don't ask." His mouth commanded her lips to part. His tongue surged forward frankly. She wasn't putting him back on any shelf.

A stunned moment drew out to a handful of riveting sensations. He'd wanted to kiss her good morning. The surprise was how badly he'd wanted it. Only one idea from last night held up in the light of day. She had to be sure with him, trusting. She had to know what kind of woman she was before he showed her what kind of woman she could be.

He reluctantly separated his mouth from hers. "I love you."

She swallowed. Nineteen days before the shuttle would return her to Earth. Nineteen days of pretending she was happy because she couldn't bear to make him unhappy. She pecked him on the nose. "I love you right back."

"Do you?" He eased his body shamelessly next to hers. "Then you should have stayed in bed, woman."

Everything melted but her resolve. "I thought breakfast would be a nicer way of saying it."

"The way to a man's heart, huh?"

"That explains why I haven't won many hearts. I had to find a man who likes prepackaged meals!" Another peck on the cheek. "Come and get it."

"Think I've already got it." He wasn't budging, his

arms and legs locked with hers. Her lunge toward the table only tilted them in midair. "I thought you'd like the hammock our first time. More normal that way."

"What would you know about normal," she teased, "when you're superior in every way?"

"Was I?"

"Adam, breakfast is served." She stared directly at him, the better to register her exasperation. A traitorous part of her soul used the chance to memorize those lines around his eyes, the shaggy hair warring with the razored sides. She ran her fingers over the strands tickling his ear and only stopped herself when she saw what her hand dared, how his eyes closed, his head bending as he breathed her name. "Maybe we did kind of rush things."

She felt his abdomen tighten. "Did we?"

Her fingers clenched in a fist. "There are consequences to any intimate act, and I think it'd be better if we faced them now. I'll only be here another nineteen days—"

As she recounted the sane, logical reasons they should cool off, Adam counted the million ways a man could be a fool. He'd been so wrapped up in wondering what he had or hadn't done for her, he'd never thought she'd worry about something as straightforward as consequences. He thought he'd explained all that.

She sat at the table as he reheated his coffee. "Speaking of consequences, you know I had a vasectomy. Years ago."

A bite-size piece of waffle tumbled off her fork, and he plucked it out of the air. He fed it to her, daring her tongue to dart out and lick a dot of syrup from his thumb. Intimacy had so many faces, and tastes, and gestures. Even an innocent act could catapult his thoughts back to the previous night, when he'd been writhing in her arms.

Hastily, she tapped her lips with a napkin and concentrated on her food. "I didn't know."

"I thought you read my medical file."

"Not *that* thoroughly."

He shrugged, watching her cheeks catch fire. "We've both been cleared by NASA's doctors. No diseases to worry about and, thanks to the vasectomy, no protection necessary."

Except the emotional kind, Maggie reminded herself. "Why?" The question shimmied out on a whisper.

"Considering what happened with Todd, I didn't want to leave Julie with another child to raise alone. It made sense at the time."

Those last words brought her gaze back to his. "Is it reversible?"

"Do you want it to be?"

The console blipped and a far-off hydraulic system hissed as the station automatically righted itself in orbit. Maggie didn't move. "I never planned on children myself."

"Never? Or since this problem came up?"

Another privilege of intimacy, coming right out and asking the question as if they knew each other well enough to discuss these issues.

"Not since I grew up with four brothers. I'm not domestic, I mentioned that."

She watched his gaze rake the waffles, the boxes of coffee and juice, the two strips of cholesterol-free bacon, the needlework place mats dishes would never adhere to.

"Yeah, right. About last night—"

How she hated those words. Her fingers instantly curled around the fork.

"I shouldn't have made all those promises about kids and houses." He trudged on. "I couldn't give you the one, and I won't be around for the other. Maybe we should make that clear."

"Please do."

"I believe in honesty."

Except where one subject was concerned, so did Maggie.

"I can't give any woman a future, but for the time being I don't see anything holding us back."

No? Maggie's eyes widened. She named half a dozen. Professionalism, duty, consequences.

He smoothly overrode them all. "It could be fun, you and me, three weeks with no other crews checking in. As long as there's nothing medical to worry about, we could throw caution to the winds."

"There is no wind in space."

He chucked her under the chin. "You're being logical again. Let it go, Maggie."

He moved to the console, signing in for the morning.

Maggie practically sputtered when she opened her mouth to argue. "So we're going to be bedmates!"

"No better way to spend our free time."

"I take it I'm more fun than the VCR."

One look at her appalled expression, and he'd already decided to drop this tactic. Pretending sex didn't matter was *not* the way to break down Maggie's inhibitions. His voice gentled. "You've got three weeks to give me memories that'll last three years."

"Mars."

"It's a long trip. I'd like to have you there with me. In my dreams. Under my skin."

Damn the man for needing her. If he was so intent on loneliness and distance, how could he ask for company? Perhaps because he knew she couldn't refuse. "Memories."

The radio crackled.

"Memories and work," Adam quipped, flicking a switch, "two things a man in space can't stay sane without. 'Morning, Mission Control."

" 'Morning, Adam. Maggie there?"

"Right here, Hal."

"As of oh-seven hundred hours, Maggie, we've got two network interviews and a call-waiting from the

Vice President. While you two were sleeping off the excitement, CNN was broadcasting an audio tape of your rescue mission."

Maggie swallowed at the phrase "you two were sleeping. . . ." No one said they were in the same bed. "Uh, thank you, Hal. I guess I could talk to them."

"You're a credit to the civilian program, Maggie. We're proud to have you aboard."

"You can say that again," Adam declared, hugging her to him in full view of the bridge camera. "Her being here made a world of difference to me."

"Then let me announce your first reward," Hal added, interrupting the long look Adam gave her. Maggie floated to attention. "The commission to design the living quarters on Outreach One, the mission to Mars, has officially been awarded to Margaret Mead Mullins. We'll transmit the diagrams so you can get to work."

"Thank you." It was something, anyway. If she couldn't give Adam the kind of love he expected, at least she could surround him with it as he flew to Mars.

The smell of dirt, water, greenery, and all that freshly produced oxygen made Maggie dizzy. She stopped in the hatchway of Botany Bay and inhaled life, real life, freed at last from the floating fishbowl of questions beamed her way over the last few days. On Earth she was something of a star. Up there only she and Adam knew the real failure.

He wanted memories. She gave him arguments.

Maggie winced as she remembered their raised voices. Perhaps he'd known all along she was faking. If not, he'd quickly guessed. What was worse, he'd insisted on talking it over. The resulting scene was as ugly as she'd feared.

"So I win," his voice had rasped through the thin

panel of the bedroom door she'd purposely shut. "I got there first, so give me a medal."

"It's not your fault."

"So it's yours."

"Who else would I blame?"

She pictured the vein in his jaw as he ground his teeth on a curse. "We're not keeping score, Maggie. Did I talk too much? Did I distract you?"

"Yes. No. Sometimes. Look, I don't want a postmortem, okay? This is precisely what I wanted to avoid."

"Are you writing everything down in there? Telling your journal what you should be telling me?"

She opened the door then, just far enough to look him in the eye. "I can't figure it out, not on paper, not with you. That's it, Adam, that's the final conclusion. When it comes to sex, I don't know what I'm doing."

He crossed his arms, claiming a long look up and down her body. She wore a simple cotton camisole, cotton panties. She hadn't dressed to seduce him— her brothers had seen her in as much.

"Answer me one question," he demanded. "Did you enjoy it?"

She gave him her best "You've gotta be kidding" look. That much at least, she couldn't hide.

He grinned, cocky and assured, and chucked her under the chin. "Then what are we arguing for?"

Moving the door aside, he raised her mouth to his, lifting her off the floor with nothing but a touch, her neck as long as a swan's as she stretched to touch her lips to his, her soul flying upward on wings.

"Ninety-nine out of a hundred things," he murmured. "Not bad for a start."

In twenty-four hours she'd missed him so much, wanting, aching, knowing it couldn't be. If these sensations were all she could have, wasn't it wiser to treasure them all the more?

"And if you enjoy this, we'll try a little more," he said, "and a little more, and before you know it—"

"Home run," she retorted, her voice flat. The wings folded; her heart plummeted to earth.

Adam strafed a hand through his hair. "What'd I say wrong now?"

"You're not here to solve my problem. Some things just are." And some women just aren't, she thought, the idea keening through her like an icy wind. "Why is it men always want to fix things?"

"Men," Adam spat out. "I'm better than any man you've slept with and you know it."

Maggie trained a shocked look his way. With one shove she propelled him into the hall and shoved the door closed. "Don't let me ruin your batting average with women!"

"Dammit, Maggie, do you *have* to do this? I want to help, and you turn it into some macho thing. I'm good, Maggie. That may be the one thing I know about women."

She hugged herself tight, fighting back the tears, blocking out his urgent strangled whispers.

"I want to be there for you, babe, is that some sin? I hate the whole idea of some other guy touching you. Or worse, of you never trying again. For all I know, that's why you joined the astronaut program. The college dorms, the prison cells, everywhere you work you make sure the men are off limits."

Her throat was so tight, her voice came out shrill. "Don't you dare analyze me, Adam Strade!"

"As I recall, you came here planning to do the same to me. You learned a few things about yourself instead."

"And you're the man to teach me."

"Yes."

She laughed, choking it off before it became a sob, staring blindly at the bedroom, the quarters she'd designed for him. "The bravest man in the universe takes on another impossible task," she said bitterly. "You're always taking on jobs that aren't yours,

Adam—raising Tad, marrying Julie. I'm not your duty."

"I never said you were."

"Then respect my fear, okay?"

"Cowardice is the one thing test pilots have no respect for," he'd shouted from behind the door. . . .

Two days later, working on her sketches for the living quarters of Outreach One, Maggie tasted tears on her tongue. Ashes too.

"Thought you'd be hiding in here."

She glanced up, blinking. A deep breath concealed a sniff. "Hello."

He drifted into the room, a towel draped around his shoulders, white against the navy polo shirt he'd tugged on. A triangle of chest hair glistened with sweat from his afternoon workout.

It was up to her to speak. "I think there should be a Botany Bay on the ship to Mars."

"Helps with the oxygen mix."

"There are psychological advantages too. Smells, sensations, earthiness."

He grunted low in his throat and his eyes darkened.

"Moisture," she said, her lips rubbing lightly on the word as her hand clenched the notepad.

"Moisture, yeah. That one always gets me."

If it wasn't a touch, it was a caress, a stroke in passing, a suggestive comment, and that hungry look. He wanted her, but bitter words hung between them.

Adam ran a hand through his hair, complaining that it was harder to manage every day. Kind of like their lives. "Do you have to hide from me, Maggie?"

"Licking my wounds, I guess."

"Let me. Lick, that is."

Her frown couldn't dampen the rush of sensation sizzling through her. Imagination was truly one of the most erogenous zones. And Adam had quite an imagination. She wondered if he tortured himself with it the way she did.

The sweat sheening on his skin answered her question. Unreleased tension had a way of gnawing, growing.

"Please," she implored.

"Please what? Please you? Give me a chance."

"Stop it."

"Start it."

"Adam."

"Eve?"

"That's right. This is your Eden, isn't it?"

"My favorite part of the station. We're the only two people on this planet."

"And we can't repopulate it."

"We can share it."

He touched her, as he had so many times over the previous days, strumming her temples when he found her hunched over her journal, working feverishly to make him the best living quarters a man could have—the home she couldn't give him, the only caring she could show.

"It's here," she said miserably, "on paper. I'll be there with you. Don't ask for any more."

"I'm asking, Maggie. Don't make me beg."

Eleven

She wouldn't be so cruel. But she couldn't be the woman he wanted. "I'm designing this for you. It's the most I can give you—please take it."

He glanced briefly at the drawing. "Is that the kind of room you'd like?"

Her heart leapt. "Me?"

"Your daring rescue has the world abuzz about women in space. Thanks to you, I might get a mixed-gender crew."

"Oh." Some woman already in training would spend three years with Adam Strade. Maggie sensed him waiting for her reaction. It took her a moment to decide what it was.

Jealousy? Envy? Images of every deadly sin found in the original garden. She despised her competition, but whose fault was it if she willingly let Adam go?

She closed her eyes and trembled, on the verge of asking him to hold her again. He wasn't asking for the moon, after all.

"I want you with me," he said, "every day and night, all the way to Mars and back."

In spirit. A memory. She grasped his wrist as he touched her face. That was real.

How could a woman who'd risked her life to save the man she loved crumble before a small hurdle? She'd fight for him before she'd hand him over to another woman, slay the dragon of her own fear, even if the lance pointed directly at her heart.

She reached out to him, as she had on the outside when a universe surrounded them. Silently she asked him to love her again.

"Give me the words, Maggie. Tell me what you want."

She gave him a kiss. "I want it fast, so fast I can't stop and think."

He got the message. The crocheted vest stretched as he tugged the buttons free. "It's the journey, not the destination," he said. "This isn't about what I think of you; it's how you feel, every step of the way. You with me?"

She nodded but stopped his lips with her fingertips. "But this is for you, something to take with you so you won't be alone."

He took her pinky in his mouth and sucked. Then her next finger. "Anything else you'd like me to do with my mouth?"

She colored like flower petals blushing open at dawn. "Not yet."

The years gaped before them. The few hours, the days they had left, would have to do. Memories couldn't be as precious as touch, taste, the scrape of his stubbled cheek, his body heated with exercise and exertion.

Her brow creased with one deep vertical as she tugged his shirt free of his waistband, her mouth pursed in determined concentration. She was doing this for him—and she was scared to death.

"Is the radio on?" she asked.

"No, we're alone." He'd just signed off, in fact, asking Hal a favor, telling him there'd be no transmissions for a while. A good long while.

He raked his lips down the side of her neck,

making sure she knew when she touched him where he liked it. He would let her concentrate on his pleasure, his arousal taking the focus off hers. "Touch me, lower."

Her hands ranged over his chest, navigating the ridges of his abdomen, the heat of him. Their bodies glided up over the foliage, the wafting ferns, the fragrant blooms. The glass barrier above them seemed frighteningly fragile—and every bit as real as the barrier Maggie longed to break through.

"Adam," she murmured. This was his Eden.

Sensations grew as she learned him, the way he shuddered when she placed her mouth on his nipple, the way desire pooled within her as they tumbled, her legs bared and his hands freely roaming their satiny length. His own satiny length, stark and powerful, throbbed urgently in her hand.

He ushered her away from danger, sending them whirling gently through the bay as he gripped her around her waist. Brazenly they rolled, revolving, swiveling through the fragrant air. No sheets to clothe them, no doors to hide them, no shame to slow them. Weighted with longing, Maggie felt her body flowing as they did, drunk on the salty tastes, the heavy aromas of fertile soil.

"Do it for me," he commanded.

Her legs effortlessly wound around him, words of praise and murmurs of delight urging her on, sweeping her up in a blur of mounting delirium. Moist and ready, she let him slip inside her. She secretly relished the stretch of intimate places, the way her body accommodated his, the risks it took.

"You feel good around me," he said.

"Don't talk."

"They're only words, Maggie. They can add to this, like memories, but they can't begin to replace the real thing." He clasped her derriere and moved her in tantalizing circles on his shaft. "Will you remember?"

She panted, her breath suddenly unruly. It didn't

respond when she asked, refusing to fill her starved lungs, her haggard attempts at speech. "Yes."

His mouth found her ear, swept it naked of its red tresses, and proceeded to murmur every coarse word he knew, primitive, explicit, relentlessly to the point. He wanted her focused on what his body did, concentrating on sensations instead of shortcomings.

It almost worked. She moaned and clutched his shoulders, arching back with no fear of falling, ardently seeking that spot, that space, that would ignite her.

He pumped and drove, surging toward the eruption that would unite them both. But in the sudden silence she listened. She thought. "So close," she whimpered, the rhythm lost. "I could almost taste it." She wrapped her arms around his neck, her face buried, hidden.

No tears, Adam vowed. Not this time. He wouldn't taste her tears again. He'd taste her.

Slipping his hands past her breasts, he wedged them under her arms, lifting her off him. She sighed in defeat. "It isn't over," he murmured. "Not until I convince you I love you."

"I know you do."

"I love this." He kissed her neck, the ridge of her collarbone. "These." The mounds of her small breasts, tight with unexpended desire. "This." Her downy belly and, finally, a fragrant tangle of red curls, damp with honey.

She gasped, stunned and suddenly modest. He clamped his hands behind her thighs, opening her again.

She quaked against him. Like fire feeding on oxygen, her desire soared. Sweat dotted her skin in an atmosphere thick with humidity. Heat flushed through her, excitement, embarrassment, no intimacy more thorough in its exposure.

Her eyes half opened; she squeezed them shut. "No, please, this isn't the way."

"Isn't it?" he demanded gruffly. "You faked it last time. Is this fake?"

She gasped. "No, please."

"Why not? Why only like this?"

She moaned and accepted his penetrating thrust, all the keener for the strumming vibrations it sent skittering inside her.

"Am I big enough, Maggie? Hard enough? Don't I fill you up?"

His insistence surprised her. Orders and blunt commands were a part of him she hadn't counted on. "You're distracting me."

"Write it down. Add it to the list of my demerits."

"Adam, stop. I won't have it like this."

His face loomed before her, his mouth jagged, his eyes dark. "Like what? Like this?"

He thrust again, and she almost cried out, a gathering swirl of stars and darkness clouding her mind. "Not angry! This isn't the way it should be." As if she knew. As if she had any idea the depths to which real love could go.

She grappled with him, unable to loosen his lock on her waist. She kicked, twisted, moving her legs every way she could to block the access he'd already gained. Her heels thudded with the hollows behind his knees, each move, each position, intensifying the sensations sweeping her under.

She bucked against him, her heart hammering. "This is no way to do this!"

His voice grated under the sound of her tiny yip as he pinched her. "You own the rules?"

"Anger has no place," she panted, "in a . . . oh my . . . physical relationship. Stop, please. This isn't a proper basis—"

He muttered his opinion of her basis. She couldn't catch her breath, couldn't right herself as they gyrated in space. Writhing in his embrace, the wall came up behind her so suddenly, it knocked the little breath remaining from her lungs.

Adam mercilessly squeezed the rest away, gripping the doorjamb, pressing her back, back, while he thrust into her. He rotated his hips in a way she could have sworn was obscene if it hadn't felt so very delicious.

Sizzling, tingling sensations erupted all over her body, signals, impulses. Maggie's eyes fluttered shut, her head weakly wavering back and forth. "No . . ."

"No basis," Adam repeated, head bowed, muscles clenched as he gripped the hatchway tighter.

"Anger and sex don't mix."

"Don't they? They're passion, Maggie."

"They shouldn't—"

"They do. Get mad, Maggie. Get even. Stop being so damn nice about all those fools who failed *you*. Resist me. Fight me. Take it, Maggie, take it."

She moved against him, with him, friction produced heat, heat passion, passion the irresistible melting, the unutterable tension, building, compelling her onward.

"Adam!"

He opened his eyes. She looked startled, teetering. He knew sensations were ricocheting through her she hadn't expected, had never experienced. A few more seconds; he had to hold on.

"Tell me you love me," he ordered. Anything to stop her noticing how close she was, anything to stop that dawning look in her eyes.

"You were trying to make me angry, trying—"

The rockets lit. The retro boosters firing right on time, shuddering the space station from stem to stern. A chute of flame erupted from the cylinders, spraying the blackness with ignited fuel, lighting the windows with reds of fire and golden heat.

Maggie gasped and quivered as the ignition sent vibrations jarring through her. Like a wave crashing against a breakwater, the ripples rumbled through her and back to him, dragging her under in a mounting thundering undulation. She quivered convulsively, meeting each frenzied thrust, crying out his name.

Minutes passed before she could breathe, think, or speak. "The ship," she murmured. "The rockets."

He wrapped her legs around his waist, keeping them joined as he let go of the wall. They floated free once again. "I promised you fireworks, didn't I?"

She tapped him on the side of the head, as if half expecting a hollow sound. "Adam, what happened?"

His grin was as cocky as the first time he'd winked at her on the monitor. "Well, when a man and a woman make love—"

"I know that. But don't you care about the station?"

"She was the most important thing in my life. Until you." He made it clear what he loved was in his arms. And that he wasn't going to waste any more time on technical questions.

"Then we're okay," Maggie said, her eyes wide as the impact of her words dawned.

"You did it, babe. We made it."

She touched him tenderly. "The station is fine."

"Everything is right as rain."

Before he could seal things with a kiss, the sprinklers mounted above Botany Bay burst into life, spurting their naked bodies with icy shards of water.

"I can't believe you did that on purpose," Maggie said with a laugh later that evening.

Adam had sputtered and cursed, hurtling through the bay to the shutoff valve, admitting after much arm-twisting from Maggie that the water had been his backup system in case the rockets had failed to distract her completely.

Returning to the bridge, it wasn't any easier explaining to Hal why their hair was wet and their uniforms dry.

But their separate evening tasks flew by, and soon

all that remained was the laughter, and one amazing memory.

Maggie sighed.

"What is it?"

"You did all that for me."

"I love you."

"Mmm." Her brave, resolute man. He knew what she needed and was determined to provide it. Duty called; he answered. "Nothing fazes you, does it? You won't let go of a goal, or a hurt, until you're satisfied."

"It was you I wanted to satisfy."

She grinned and cuddled closer in the zippered hammock.

Adam slid a fingertip over one of her more accessible erogenous zones. "Had to get your mind off yourself and your problems and me and my expectations."

"Distracting me with anger was part of that."

"Elementary psychology."

"And the retro-rockets?"

"More fun than a vibrating bed."

"We'll have to try one of those. Someday."

Someday. As if life on Earth would be a continuation of their unusual situation. As if Adam weren't leaving for Mars. For once, the timetable mattered to Maggie. She'd be on Earth one month before Adam came back down. Eight to ten months after that he would be ready to leave on his three-year voyage.

Adam tucked a kiss behind her ear and gave her another excuse to sigh.

They'd already made long, delectable love, the cumulative result of an evening spent barely keeping their hands to themselves under the watchful eye of Mission Control. Maggie had sat anxiously through a live network broadcast answering each of the interviewer's questions, neatly sidestepping leading remarks about the man she'd saved. There was no denying an expression of love the entire world had heard.

She'd practically slapped his hand as he'd patted her in a place the camera couldn't see.

"Think we'll always need good vibrations?" she asked later, wrinkling her nose at the question.

Adam shook his head, the hammock swaying with the motion. "We didn't a few minutes ago."

"No." The wonder hadn't worn off. It was a most amazing discovery, something that only worked when a man cared enough to put her pleasure first.

Their murmurs sounded in the small room. The ship was as empty as ever, humming along on its orbital path, a path Adam spent an hour correcting after that rocket blast. And yet, drifting thousands of miles above the nearest planet, it felt filled with love, a true home.

"How much time?" Maggie asked, knowing the sentence didn't need finishing, knowing the numbers as well as he.

"Crandall arrives in two and a half weeks. You go back when his crew does. I train him up here for a month, then come down myself with the next shuttle crew. Grigg wants to study how much bone I've lost in the sixteen months I've been up here. That'll be three months on the ground at least."

"I could tell him about your bones." Maggie chuckled.

"To think you were a demure lady scientist when you arrived barely a month ago."

"And here I am bare again. Fancy that."

Her touch made him groan.

"Give me at least another fifteen minutes, hon. I'm not the man I used to be."

No, she thought with a smile, he was no longer a man alone. They'd both changed. They loved now, openly and completely, accepting each other into their solitary lives. "And then?"

"After Grigg there'll be Hal and choosing the crew. I know one of them; the other two spots are open."

"And us?"

"A year maybe."

He was exaggerating, she knew.

"You know NASA," he explained unnecessarily. "They're going to be careful as all get out. If they postpone lift-off less than twice, I'll be surprised."

"And if they're on time, you'll be gone in eight months."

They reached for each other in the milky starlight of the cabin. The impressive safety record of all the shuttle flights might tempt one to overlook the danger. Maggie needed to look no further than the woman this space station was named for to remember accidents happened.

Adam stroked her arm. "I'll be fine."

"I know." That wouldn't make it easier. Would missing him hurt less in three years? Her heart was as silent as the ship and the empty heavens around them.

At least she could love him. Fill those silent, distant years to come with memories they'd both cherish.

Three angry days had once seemed an eternity on the station. The next sixteen flew by so fast, Maggie wanted to call them back. She and Adam made love. They laughed. They told each other stories of their childhood, their lives. They watched movies that never got finished, ate popcorn that seemed to continually float away because their hands were busy elsewhere.

They fell in love each night. And again each morning.

Adam taught her everything her body could do. Her heart taught her how much leaving him would hurt.

When Hal announced Adam's official promotion to

flight commander on the mission to Mars, they celebrated. And in the dark they wept.

"Take me with you," she begged.

"I can't." He could take her to the stars, hold her in his heart, possess her in his bed. None of it eased the ache of their coming separation.

"It's only for a month," he insisted as they sat side by side, watching the lift-off of Max Crandall's shuttle live from Cape Canaveral.

Adam made a promise, for once guaranteeing an outcome he knew he couldn't control. "I'll be back," he vowed. Back to Earth in a month, back from Mars in three years.

If only she'd wait.

Five days later Adam was the one glued to the console, watching the returning shuttle circling Edwards Air Force Base as it prepared to touch down with America's favorite woman astronaut aboard.

There had been disastrous lift-offs in the past. Never a bad landing. Adam closed his eyes and kept that in mind.

"Looking forward to terra firma?" Crandall asked, clamping his hand on Adam's shoulder.

"Yeah," he grunted, listening impatiently to the vacuous reassurances of television newscasters. Edwards was crawling with media wanting to welcome America's sweetheart—the woman he loved.

"—miss her too," Crandall said.

"Huh?"

"If I had a woman like that, I'd miss her too." His gray eyes were riveted on Adam.

"Tell me Hal doesn't know," Adam muttered, running a hand over his face.

Max merely smiled. "I think Hal's known since day one. He didn't like the idea of you being up here alone too long."

"Don't tell me he actually believed those rumors about me cracking up!"

"Matter of fact, I think he started them. Great excuse to get Maggie up here. He saw the sparks you two struck chatting on the big screen."

Adam clenched his jaw before his mouth could drop open. "I winked at her, for crying out loud!"

Max shrugged. "Maybe he figured it was time to coax you back from your self-imposed exile. Since you wouldn't come down, he sent someone up."

"Do scientists ever stop playing God?" Adam mumbled.

"Maybe he thought you needed a rib." Max slapped him on the back, bounding backward with an astonished curse. "Whoa! Haven't got the hang of this yet."

Adam laughed. Distractions had their uses. He ought to know. His gut tightened as he watched the screen again. The shuttle was coming in. "How's your pilot?"

"I'd be at the controls myself if I was aboard."

A man after his own heart, Adam thought. But that didn't answer his question.

"Joe'll get her down safely."

Neither needed to specify which *her* Max referred to.

"Hal, may I show you those designs?"

Maggie trailed after the director of Mission Control lugging a leather case filled with layouts. For a month she'd felt draggy and slow, drugged by the stifling Houston heat, nauseated by the air-conditioning.

Mission Control's atmosphere was antiseptically run by the same system as Space Station McAuliffe. It may have kept the computers free of dust, but it lacked the delightful floating quality that made an inhuman atmosphere tolerable. It also lacked plants. And Adam Strade.

Maggie forced him out of her mind; now wasn't the

time. She'd just finished talking to him on the monitor, as she did every afternoon when he orbited directly over Texas.

Each day after Max Crandall summed up his reports, he turned the transmission over to Adam, who'd requested her as his contact. There she sat, next to Hal, relaying messages via satellite.

Adam winked at her. Called her *doll*. Asked how she was doing in a voice that made the hairs on the back of her neck stand up. Hal tugged his tie until the knot was taut. Maggie could have sworn no one looked directly at her until each day's transmission was complete.

"Bye, babe. See you next orbit." Adam's signature sign-off. It was fast becoming a national catch-phrase.

There was no way to ask him to stop it without the entire control room hearing, not to mention the lurking media.

"So tell your cheeks to stop sending blood to your capillaries!" she insisted silently, her face a telltale pink.

She wanted him back. She hadn't known how badly until the shuttle going up to fetch him was delayed by rain in Florida. Rain. She couldn't think of it, couldn't stand under a shower, without remembering the botany lab, Adam's hands all over her, their delighted laughter and charged silence as they floated free in a scheduled downpour.

That's what space was, Maggie thought, freedom. Release. Unutterable vastnesses made bearable by the addition of one person and one person only.

Hal cleared his throat. He'd been standing behind his desk all the time while Maggie gazed out the Plexiglas wall of his office on to the control room floor. Max Crandall floated across the large screen, describing docking procedures for the delayed shuttle that would return Adam Strade to Earth.

"You had something to show me, Maggie?"

Maggie was afraid he'd just seen it. She loved Adam Strade. She had no intention of letting him go off into deepest space alone *or* with strangers. "These designs." She unlatched the case and slipped out page after page of bays, rooms, dividers, fabrics.

She had calculations. Books full. She couldn't seem to sleep normal hours anymore, so she worked. She evaluated how many inches a man required from door to desk, from console to ceiling, from room to room. What would make him comfortable, never crowded or cramped, never totally alone.

She launched into her sales pitch. "Ergonomics began when the Air Force decreed a pilot couldn't be over six foot four because he'd be too big for the cockpit. I'm interested in more than work-space efficiency. It's the psychology of comfort, of feeling at home, that's vital when people are cooped up in a capsule. In fact, I believe it was my psychology degree that originally led you to send me up there."

Hal didn't say yes or no. Hal rarely said anything as straightforward as yes or no. "You have yet to file an actual report on Commander Strade's mental health."

"He's fine."

"He seemed a little melancholy these last few weeks."

He's missing me. "He's leaving a place he's made home."

"Think he'll find a new one here? Some men would give up even Mars for a normal life, if the right woman came along."

Maggie rebelled at the very suggestion. She wouldn't deprive Adam of his dream. Yes, she wanted to marry him; she longed to spend every day of her life with him. But he'd never know that.

She loved him too much to ask that of him.

Unfortunately, she loved him too intensely to sit and wait for three years. One month had almost killed her. She was a walking zombie, a workaholic ragamuffin wandering through NASA headquarters as if it were one empty warehouse after another. Earth was as lonely as space without Adam there.

"Hal, your assigning me to Space Station McAuliffe was a prize beyond imagining. I know I have no right to ask for more when there are other scientists, other astronauts . . ."

Her throat constricted; her lungs balked. She took a deep breath and, very calmly, very sincerely, looked Hal in the eye and asked for the moon, the stars, all of it. "I want to go to Mars."

Twelve

Adam knocked on the door. Maggie's heart reverberated like a tin drum. She slowly crossed the room.

No one had to tell her it was he. She'd watched the shuttle land from the safety of her living room TV, watched the hero's welcome, and the look that had crossed Adam's face when he'd searched the crowd and hadn't found her in it.

A month had passed since then. She'd worked day and night while Adam recovered from space, anticipating and dreading this day.

"Maggie." He gave a short nod as she opened the door. A frown line creased his brow. Those eyes, so capable of sizing her up at a glance, chose to examine her apartment first.

As in space, oxygen was suddenly rare and hard to come by. Maggie waved her arm as he stepped inside. "It's blank, I know."

"Pardon?" His back was to her as he walked to the middle of the room.

"I said it's blank. You were probably wondering why a woman who designs living spaces can't keep her own apartment clean and cheerful." She ran out of breath at the end of the sentence, croaking the word *cheerful*.

"I wasn't, but thanks for the rundown."

Maggie crossed her arms. Okay, so she'd chattered inanely. Someone who overanalyzed things couldn't be blamed for criticizing her own apartment.

Adam walked around the room, keeping his thoughts to himself. It was as if he carried space with him, distance, a cocoon of emptiness.

Maggie suddenly had the piercing sensation he was going to say good-bye. He'd named the third crew member for Mars; one more and the mission would be set. He'd probably come to tell her the fourth person's name. To make a final good-bye.

She couldn't ask him to stay, not in her apartment, not on Earth. "Would you like some sun tea?"

"Sun tea," he repeated, putting the two words together. "You know, I've been in the sun every minute I can steal from Grigg and his pokers and prodders. Feels good, doesn't it? On the skin, I mean."

She quivered at his level look, the possibilities behind his words. "Yes."

"The Earth feels good."

Did it? She hadn't really noticed.

"I missed you, Maggie."

"I couldn't make it to the ceremony. I'm sorry."

"Not that kind of missing." For a month he'd damned near eaten himself alive with worry while Hal fed him crumbs: Maggie was okay; Maggie was out of quarantine; Maggie was busy designing Outreach One.

All he knew was Maggie wasn't there to greet him, wasn't anywhere to be found at Mission Control.

Maggie was avoiding him. Maybe Maggie wanted to say good-bye.

Right now she was in the kitchen knocking a pitcher against glasses. Adam winced at the sound of breaking glass.

"No problem," she trilled, "it's all in the sink. I'll just clean it up and be out in a minute."

He sunk his hands in his pockets and cleared his throat. "They beamed up that TV segment on your family reunion," he called. "All your brothers, their kids, your dad and step-mom. Looked like a nice picnic."

"There were more cameras than ants, but it was fun."

"You're close to your family." Could he really ask her to give them up and go with him? Could he be so selfish?

She bumped the saloon doors with her hip and strode across the room, his glass extended. "We all travel around so much, it's nice to get together when we can."

He sipped and considered. Mars wasn't exactly a honeymoon month in Paris. It was too far, too long a trip. She'd turn him down.

"Too tart?" she asked. "Would you like sugar?"

"No, it's fine." He wiped the grimace off his face.

Maggie smiled—at her wedge of lemon. She ought to, she'd almost sliced off two fingers cutting it. "So you're back."

"For now."

"Getting used to terra firma?"

His eyes narrowed. "Thought it might be fun to try mattress firma, if you know what I mean."

She laughed and shook a finger at him. "A billboard on Memorial Parkway couldn't make it clearer."

"Good. Thought if I got too subtle it might go right over your head." He made a sweeping motion over his.

Maggie's mouth formed a perfect "Oh." "You cut your hair!"

"Actually, no. I had a real barber do it for a change."

"A military one."

"Is it too short?"

"No." She just wondered why it had taken her so long to notice. The height difference had caught her attention first; there was none. She was five ten to his five ten. In space it never mattered. On Earth it sometimes did, helping her feel gawky and unfeminine with most men. Adam didn't seem to care a whit about inches.

And his skin, she'd noticed that. The healthy tan, the crinkles, the eyes. She'd never forgotten his eyes.

He ducked his head and scruffed the short layers, inviting her to do the same. She reached up and tentatively touched it.

"The barber gave me some tips on how to keep it manageable when I'm gone."

When I'm *gone,*" *not* we. The choice of crew was up to Adam. Or so Hal had reminded her when she'd pleaded for the assignment. She noticed he wasn't asking.

"I used to trim my brothers' hair," Maggie said, casting around for the subject. "Eventually they got too big."

"Make 'em slouch in a chair."

"Height wasn't the problem." She immediately wished she hadn't brought it up. Adam's eyes scanned her top to bottom, then slowly back up.

His mouth quirked in a smile. "You were saying?"

Her heart had been beating, too, until all of three seconds before. "If they didn't like the cut, they'd chase me around the house and tickle me."

"Tickling," he mused. "Never thought of that one. Think that could work as a sexual distraction, at the proper moment, I mean?"

"No." Her eyes grew wide as saucers. "No!"

"An experiment. Purely scientific."

"No!" She backed around the sofa, edging her way between the cushions and the coffee table, warding him off with one hand. "You behave."

"I'll tell Hal you're being uncooperative."

"Don't you dare."

He shrugged and slid his hands in his jeans pockets as if giving up, then lunged when she least expected it.

Maggie hadn't been raised with boys for nothing. She squeaked and darted around the coffee table, turning just in time to see Adam sway.

"What is it?"

He gripped the flimsy maple table, bending his head to knee height. "Dizzy."

She stopped a cautious three feet away. "For real or just kidding?"

He glanced up and grinned. "Always thinking, Magpie."

"Brothers. I know the tricks."

"Yeah, well . . ." This wasn't a trick. His skin was gray under the tan, his upper lip dotted with sweat.

"You get in here." With a no-nonsense grip on his shoulders, she steered him toward the bedroom.

"Taking the initiative." He laughed weakly. "That's good."

It had taken him a week to learn to walk without lurching like a drunken sailor. The air felt like water, ponderous and so sultry, it was almost navigable. Like Frankenstein's monster, he shuffled one cumbersome foot in front of the other.

"What did Grigg say about this?" Maggie demanded.

"He said sixteen months is a long time to be without gravity."

And three years was a long time to be away from the person you loved, Maggie thought.

With one pointed finger she pushed him back on the bed. He sank with a sloshing sound.

"A water bed!"

"It's the only way I can sleep anymore," she replied. "Closest thing to sleeping in space."

"Do you miss it up there?"

All the time. Brusquely, she yanked the pillow out from under his head and put it beneath his feet.

"You joining me, Maggie?"

The question she'd been longing to hear, but not the context. "Let's get the blood flowing properly first." She picked up his foot, tugged off his boot, and began massaging his toes.

A soft moan greeted her efforts. "I'm asking, babe."

An undertow of desire shivered through her. Sensations quivered over her skin like night breezes. She'd missed breezes. Not as much as she'd missed Adam.

"Maggie, touch me."

She was. But not that way, not yet. She hauled off his other boot, massaged his arch, his ankle, his calf. His jeans were worn white, more in some places than others. There was a tear above his left knee, a bulge at the juncture of his thighs.

"Nice jeans," she said. "Wear 'em much longer, and they'll be indecent."

"You could patch them."

"I'm no good with a needle."

"No? I thought we'd proved once and for all you were a wonderful woman."

"That doesn't mean I sew."

"Then how about showing me where the weak spots are?"

Her weakest spot was Adam Strade lying prone in her bed.

He threw one arm dashingly across his forehead, his eyes firmly shut. She'd have to touch him to demonstrate. "You've got a tear here," she said.

He moaned and lifted his knee. The water undulated beneath them as he shifted his hips. "Is that all?"

"This thigh is kind of threadbare." The material might be, never the thigh. Her hand skimmed the bunched muscles under the thin fabric, the heat of his skin coming through. She lifted her hand as if scorched.

"Anywhere else?" he asked.

There was a loose metal stud at the corner of a pocket. A thread at the bottom of the zipper. A belt loop was all but torn away. Her fingers glided over the cool metal of a belt buckle tooled with a rocket design. It reminded her of a country song he'd played in space, something about *burning like a rocket.*

Her throat grew tight. "Still dizzy?" she asked.

He opened his eyes and gave her a penetrating stare, part challenge part patience. "You stopping there?"

No use pretending she hadn't touched him before, hadn't curled her fingers around him in every way he liked, any way he asked. She traced the fold of fabric over his zipper, and he covered her hand with the steady pressure of his.

"Believe it or not, Maggie, I didn't plan on falling in bed with you the minute I came back."

He'd been back a month; it was kind of him not to mention it. "I figured you'd need time to adjust. Apparently you do."

"That's not all I need."

She wanted to tell him she loved him and always would. He must have known it. Otherwise how could he ask her to touch him in his quiet, commanding voice?

"Anywhere, Maggie."

He sucked in his stomach as she jerked the T-shirt free of his belt. She had the buckle to contend with, the zipper. Things had to be slid down and tossed away. Unlike in space, clothes actually landed on the floor and stayed there.

She paused when it came time to remove her blouse. Her breasts were too small to sag; she wasn't worried about that kind of gravity. It was the opening, the revealing. They'd had an Eden, an idyll, a distant getaway. Now it was real.

She flicked the buttons out of their holes as fast as her trembling hands allowed. She couldn't coerce him with love, with promises or emotional demands; she couldn't use the moment to ask him to take her to Mars. And she couldn't wait for him if he left her behind.

Adam stalled her hands, parting the fabric himself. "Worried?" he asked, sensing her wayward thoughts.

She shook her head, her hair swaying softly across her shoulders.

"It'll work here just like it did there, babe." The weight of his hand on her thigh held an extra dimension of possessiveness as he coaxed her into bending toward him, bringing her breasts to skim against his chest, her lips to taste his.

He tasted like coffee, a mint, a man.

"You're thinking," he warned. "Thinking gets you in trouble."

"You, Adam Strade, have gotten me in more trouble than any ten men ever could."

He probed her sweet center, eliciting a swift intake of breath. "Glad you remembered."

She remembered everything he'd taught her and everything they'd done. How calmly she'd set out to save him that night on the space walk. His trust when he'd reached for her hand. It was a love to last centuries, the kind an immortal man deserved. How could she let him go now?

"Maggie," he whispered, softly trailing his lips from her ear to her throat to that warm dark place shadowed by her breast. She shivered. Her reaction didn't stop him from taking her in his mouth and sucking until she moaned. "Miss me?"

He had no right to ask such a question at the moment. His touch ignited her instantly, compelled her, luring her with promises no other man could ever fulfill—because there was no other man like Adam Strade. The original Adam, the only man she'd ever love.

She kissed him and kissed him, his forehead, lashes, those ragged brows he used to such effect when he was feeling bearish, grumpy, fixing her with a go-away look she'd learned never to take seriously.

"What's this?" His thumb brushed the moist trail of a tear.

"I'll miss you, that's all."

"Do we have to talk about it?"

They could pretend they were aloft, that no one and nothing could interfere. They could lie. "Adam . . ."

"Mag, I know what you're going to say."

Yes, Hal had probably told him the fool she'd made of herself. She'd done everything but beg to go to Mars. In the end she'd done that too.

She'd used every rule in every book about women standing up for themselves. A woman's presence was necessary on Outreach One, she'd insisted. She quoted the French crew, cited the media and her newfound fame. She'd analyzed it to death. She'd also used her heart as well as her brain.

The man needed a woman, she concluded. Sacajawea to his Lewis and Clark, Cleopatra to his Marc Antony. Name the story; she'd name the heroine. Name the man; she'd name the woman who stood beside him.

But Hal wasn't buying.

And Adam still hadn't asked.

In the slanted light of late afternoon she glimpsed the circles beneath his eyes. "You haven't been sleeping."

"You either."

"It's hard getting used to a bed."

"Harder to be alone."

Is that what he was preparing her for? Leaving? "I love you, Adam."

"Your family too."

"Not the same way. I missed you."

"You saw me every day on the video."

Her look said it wasn't the same; it would never be enough. "Are you going to send me messages from Mars?"

"I hadn't planned on it."

She died a little, pieces of her heart breaking off like brittle asteroids being flung into space. "On the space station we made memories. On Earth we're making good-byes."

She was sending him away. Adam knew it as surely as if she'd written it on his skin with her nails. Maybe six weeks in space had been enough; taking her with him was just a pipe dream.

He caught her arms in his as she tried to sit up. "Maggie, let me make love to you. Now, before we say anything else."

He stroked her body with his hand, learning what he already knew, marking what was already his.

What started tenderly ended with rapid desperation. She took, it was all she could do, stunned at his energy, his sudden hunger. When he said, "Come with me," only she knew what his special plea meant. With him she was the woman she'd always wanted to be, giving as a woman could, daring it all. No other woman, none, could love him the way she had. None could fly with him among the stars.

She kissed his chest, her lips trembling, her desire fulfilled but still unquenched. It wasn't enough. There wasn't time enough in the universe to say good-bye to Adam Strade, to find all the words that would have to remain unsaid.

His chest expanded as she rested her cheek against it. His arm lay heavy on her back. "There were times when I got so lonely with you gone, I thought of never going up again."

Her breath stopped in her lungs. "Don't say that."

"Do you want me to go?"

Not now. Not ever. She rolled off the bed, her feet hitting the floor with a thud. Grabbing a robe from the closet, she strode into the living room. She couldn't fall apart, couldn't burst into tears and ask him to give up his dream. It wasn't a memory she'd send him away with; a woman had her pride.

In a moment his steps sounded behind her, measured, steady. Her heart ached to think she'd never heard them before, might never hear them again.

"This is no time to walk away, Maggie."

"Isn't it? You're leaving, and I can't make you stay."

"You haven't tried."

Her eyes were bright with tears, the paperwork strewn across her desk a blurry mess she couldn't blink away. "I could ask you to give it all up for me."

"Why don't you?"

"Because you might say yes. I won't ask that of you."

He smiled, a sad, rueful cant of his mouth. "Or I might say no."

She laughed, wiping a tear with the corner of her sleeve. "Maybe that's what I'm really afraid of. You know me, if I don't write it down, I have no idea what I'm feeling."

"You can tell me."

"I could."

She loved him; he knew that as surely as he knew the Earth revolved around the sun. But she loved her family too. Loved Earth. This would be so much easier if one of them ended it, drew the line. He couldn't do it. His brave Maggie was the one with the guts.

"I could ask you to wait for me," he said, waiting rigidly for her reply.

Her voice was unexpectedly small. "I didn't really expect you to."

"No? Then you don't expect enough." He grasped her chin, pulling her mouth to his. It wasn't so easy with her feet firmly on the ground, not half as graceful as in space.

But style wasn't the point. Spirals of desire whirled through them both, rugged and raw, unrefined. His tongue found her teeth, her open, yielding mouth, and took, and took some more.

They came up gasping, rough panted breaths passing between them, their foreheads resting hard against each other. "You think I'd let you get away?" he asked harshly.

"Sometimes a man has bigger dreams."

"More important than you, you mean."

"More important than anything," she said. "Adam, you could be immortal; you could be a hero."

"I'm not now?"

She quirked her mouth into a smile. "To me, yes. I mean to the world."

"Yeah, right, the greatest hero who ever left the woman he loved." And the biggest bastard.

He was done using space as a hiding place. But the explorer's instincts remained, the dream. He'd given up the prospect of children to chase it. Could he sacrifice a wife too? Lose a once-in-a-lifetime love for a first in the history books?

"I won't stand in the way of your dreams, Adam."

"Then you'll wait."

Looking in the eyes of the man she loved was the most difficult thing Maggie had ever done. She shook her head. "This last month was harder than I ever imagined. I don't think I'd survive three years. Maybe it'd be better if we ended things now."

Her heart skittered to a stop as he dropped his hands from her arms.

He stepped away, studying the designs littering the surface of her desk, watercolors and tinted drawings she'd labored over lovingly, far into the night. Too many times she'd caught herself staring out the window at the stars, the red planet on the horizon just before dawn. She'd stared at the moon, jealous of a lifeless oversized asteroid because it was closer to him than she was.

"You've doubled the size of my cabin."

"It seemed kind of crowded."

"I liked it that way." He'd liked it with her in it.

He turned and scanned the room, the blank walls, the serviceable furniture. "My quarters are more of a home than this place is. Is that your going-away present?"

She twisted away, cheeks coloring.

"Hal said—"

"What did he say?" she asked tightly.

He said Adam couldn't use their relationship as a lever, couldn't bribe her to join the mission. Even Hal couldn't order a woman to spend three years in space if she didn't want to. It was up to her to volunteer, to leave the Earth, her home, everything but the man she loved.

"It's going to be a great ship," Adam said. "Hard to believe you did all this when you knew you'd never experience it yourself. You're a caring woman."

No, she wasn't. She was selfish and conniving, and every drawing practically shouted that fact. Couldn't he see she wanted to be on that ship?

"I know you never believed me when I said this before. You're a wonderful woman, Maggie."

She believed him now because she ached like one, because she was loved every bit as fiercely. "Adam, I won't wait here while you're gone."

"I know, babe, get it over with if you have to."

"I didn't learn how to love so I could lose you!"

"Then ask me to stay."

"No!" She swiped the drawings off the desk and over the floor. "You're going to be Neil Armstrong, Charles Lindbergh, and Christopher Columbus all rolled into one. Except your boat won't leak and your crew won't mutiny, I'll see to that."

He laughed hollowly. "How?"

"Bring me along."

Oblivious to her strangled plea, Adam crouched over the drawings, especially the one of the bedroom. To hell with Hal's rules. If she didn't want to come along, she'd just have to look him in the eye and tell him so.

"You know, a psychologist on board is a great idea," he began. "A woman with your experience would fit right in, know how to ease the tensions."

Maggie threw her hands in the air and hurled the

words at his obstinate back. "What do you think I've been pestering Hal about the last two months!"

Adam slowly stood. "You what?"

For seconds Maggie wished she were shorter, taller; anything would be better than experiencing his implacable eye-to-eye stare. But first she had to find her voice, the one that still reverberated around the underfurnished room. "I can't watch you go, and I can't ask you to stay. I want to go with you."

"Why didn't you say so earlier?"

Damn the man! How could he be so infuriatingly calm? "Because Hal told me I couldn't use your love to coerce you!"

"And he told *me* you had to volunteer." Adam reached around her waist and reeled her in tight. "I think Hal has a lot to answer for."

"So do I."

Light began to dawn, flickers of starlight in her hazel eyes. They both smiled, then laughed, holding each other close.

"You want to go with me?"

"Always."

Adam tucked her head against his shoulder, anchoring it there with his chin. "If you weren't sick and tired of space and ready to send me packing, why haven't you been down to Mission Control for the last month?"

"I've had all this work." She nodded toward the paper-covered floor.

"And?" Adam gave her another squeeze. "And, Maggie?"

"I was afraid you wouldn't ask me."

"I'm not."

"Oh?" She knew that bearish scowl. It was her turn to sling her arms around his neck and sidle up to him, hip to hip, robe falling immodestly open. "Commander, after all we've been through, you're not inviting me to Mars?"

"I'm ordering you. You're coming with me, if I have

to strap you across my lap in the command module."

"You mean a real live space raider is going to steal me away to a far-off planet?"

"And love you until the stars revolve in the heavens. Yes, Maggie, yes."

They kissed, long and sweet and slow, the weight of gravity drawing them down, two lovers entwined in the streaming rays of the evening sun.

"Gran will have to knit me another sweater."

"Make it two. We'll be gone a long time."

"But we'll be together." She kissed him playfully, joyfully, gratefully. She'd caught his hand again, and this time she'd never let go.

"Ready?" Maggie slipped a cassette in the VCR and snuggled next to Adam on the sofa cushions.

They were one year into the journey to Mars, six months from actually reaching the planet. There were astronomical charts to monitor, experiments to conduct, and two other crew members to coordinate with. Maggie made sure everyone and everything ran smoothly, satisfied that her work on people in space would be a landmark for explorers setting out on even longer missions in the future.

Adam steered the ship, communicated with an ever-farther Houston, and conducted all the maintenance. He liked to joke that Outreach One was an immensely complex and incredibly expensive starter home.

"Where's Major Wells?" Maggie asked, settling in for the evening.

"Sleeping before his shift on the bridge."

"Lieutenant Reed?"

"Working in the botany lab. We've got three hours. Get over here on my lap."

"Aye, aye, sir."

Adam held her near. A slow, deep kiss of welcome

greeted her, a promise of more to come. "Ready," he finally said.

She pushed the button.

A whir and a flicker, then an announcer intoned, "This is the Evening News."

"Good evening," the anchorman said. "Tonight, we lead with an out-of-this-world romance. To the surprise of few and the delight of many, Commander Adam Strade and Astronaut Margaret Mead Mullins were married today in a ceremony performed by an Air Force chaplain in Houston and transmitted via satellite to the orbiting pair.

"Strade and Mullins are stopping over on Space Station McAuliffe for a few days before their final journey begins toward the red planet, Mars. Champagne was uncorked at Mission Control as cheers resounded through the airwaves and beyond. . . ."

"Happy anniversary, Adam."

"Happy anniversary, darling."

"Till the Earth stops spinning—"

"—and the stars burn away. I love you, Maggie."

THE EDITOR'S CORNER

What an irresistible line-up of romance reading you have coming your way next month. Truly, you're going to be **LOVESWEPT** by these stories that are guaranteed to heat your blood and keep you warm throughout the cold, winter days ahead.

First on the list is **WINTER BRIDE**, LOVESWEPT #522, by the ever-popular Iris Johansen. Ysabel Belfort would trade Jed Corbin anything for his help on a perilous mission—her return to her South American island home, to recover what she'd been forced to leave behind. But he demands her sensual surrender, arousing her with a fierce pleasure, until they're engulfed in a whirlwind of danger and desire. . . . A gripping and passionate love story, from one of the genre's premier authors.

You'll be **BEWITCHED** by Victoria Leigh's newest LOVESWEPT, #523, as Hank Alton is when he meets Sally. According to his son, who tried to steal her apples, she's a horribly ugly witch, but instead Hank discovers a reclusive enchantress whose eyes shimmer with warmth and mystery. A tragedy had sent Sally Michaels in search of privacy, but Hank shatters her loneliness with tender caresses and burning kisses. Victoria gives us a shining example of the power of love in this touching romance guaranteed to bring a smile to your face and tears to your eyes.

Judy Gill creates a **GOLDEN WARRIOR**, LOVESWEPT #524, in Eric Lind, for he's utterly masculine, outrageously sexy, and has a rake's reputation to match! But Sylvia Mathieson knows better than to get lost in his bluer-than-blue eyes. He claims to need the soothing fire of her love, and she aches to feel the heat of his body against hers, but could a pilot who roams the skies ever choose to make his home in her arms? The sensual battles these two engage in will keep you turning the pages of this fabulous story from Judy.

Please give a big welcome to brand-new author Diane Pershing and her first book, **SULTRY WHISPERS,** LOVESWEPT #525. Lucas Barabee makes Hannah Green melt as he woos her with hot lips and steamy embraces. But although she wants the job he offered, she knows only too well the danger of mixing business with pleasure. You'll delight in the sweet talk and irresistible moves Lucas must use to convince Hannah she can trust him with her heart. A wonderful romance by one of our New Faces of '92!

In **ISLAND LOVER,** LOVESWEPT #526, Patt Bucheister sweeps you away to romantic Hawaii, where hard-driving executive Judd Stafford has been forced to take a vacation. Still, nothing can distract him . . . until he meets Erin Callahan. Holding her is like riding a roller coaster of emotions—all ups and downs and stomach-twisting joy. But Erin has fought hard for her independence, and she isn't about to make it easy for Judd to win her over. This love story is a treat, from beginning to end!

Laura Taylor has given her hero quite a dilemma in **PROMISES,** LOVESWEPT #527. Josh Wyatt has traveled to the home he's never known, intending to refuse the inheritance his late grandfather has left him, but executor Megan Montgomery is determined to change his mind. A survivor and a loner all his life, Josh resists her efforts, but he can't ignore the inferno of need she arouses in him, the yearning to experience how it feels to be loved at last. Laura has outdone herself in crafting a story of immense emotional impact.

Look for four spectacular books this month from FAN-FARE. Bestselling author Nora Roberts will once again win your praise with **CARNAL INNOCENCE,** a riveting contemporary novel where Caroline Waverly learns that even in a sleepy town called Innocence, secrets have no place to hide, and in the heat of steamy summer night it takes only a single spark to ignite a deadly crime of passion. Lucy Kidd delivers **A ROSE WITHOUT THORNS,** a compelling historical romance set in eighteenth-century England. Susannah Bry's world is turned upside-down when her father sends her to England to live with wealthy relatives, and she meets the bold and dashing actor Nicholas Carrick. New author Alexandra Thorne will dazzle you with the contemporary novel **DESERT HEAT**. In a world of fiery beauty, lit by a scorching desert sun, three very different women will dare to seize their dreams of glory . . . and irresistible love. And, Suzanne Robinson will captivate you with **LADY GALLANT**, a thrilling historical romance in the bestselling tradition of Amanda Quick and Iris Johansen. A daring spy in Queen Mary's court, Eleanora Becket meets her match in Christian de Rivers, a lusty, sword-wielding rogue, who has his own secrets to keep, his own enemies to rout—and his own brand of vengeance for the wide-eyed beauty whom he loved too well. Four terrific books from FANFARE, where you'll find only the best in women's fiction.

Happy Reading!

With warmest wishes for a new year filled with the best things in life,

Nita Taublib

Nita Taublib
Associate Publisher / LOVESWEPT
Publishing Associate / FANFARE

Enter Loveswept's Wedding Contest

AH! WEDDINGS! The joyous ritual we cherish in our hearts—the perfect ending to courtship. Brides in exquisite white gowns, flowers cascading from glorious bouquets, handsome men in finely tailored tuxedos, butterflies in stomachs, nervous laughter, music, tears, and smiles. . . . AH! WEDDINGS!! But not all weddings have a predictable storybook ending; sometimes they are much, much more—grooms who faint at the altar, the cherubic ring bearer who drops the band of gold in the lake to see if it will float, traffic jams that strand the bride miles from the church, or the gorgeous hunk of a best man who tempts the bride almost too far. . . . AGHH!! WEDDINGS!!!

LOVESWEPT is celebrating the joy of weddings with a contest for YOU. And true to LOVESWEPT's reputation for innovation, this contest will have THREE WINNERS. Each winner will receive a year of free LOVESWEPTs and the opportunity to discuss the winning story with a LOVESWEPT editor.

Here's the way it goes. We're looking for short wedding stories, real or from your creative imagination, that will fit in one of three categories:

1) THE MOST ROMANTIC WEDDING
2) THE FUNNIEST THING THAT EVER HAPPENED AT A WEDDING
3) THE WEDDING THAT ALMOST WASN'T

This will be LOVESWEPT's first contest in some time for writers and aspiring writers, and we are eagerly anticipating the discovery of some terrific stories. So start thinking about your favorite real-life wedding experiences—or the ones you always wished (or feared?) would happen. Put pen to paper or fingers to keyboard and tell us about those WEDDINGS (AH)!!

For prizes and rules, please see rules, which follow.

BANTAM LOVESWEPT WEDDING CONTEST
OFFICIAL RULES

1. *No purchase necessary.* Enter Bantam's LOVESWEPT WEDDING CONTEST by completing the Official Entry Form below (or handprinting the required information on a plain 3" x 5" card) and writing an original story (5–10 pages in length) about one of the following three subjects: (1) The Most Romantic Wedding, (2) The Funniest Thing That Ever Happened at a Wedding, or (3) The Wedding That Almost Wasn't. Each story must be typed, double spaced, on plain 8 1/2" x 11" paper, and must be headed on the top of the first page with your name, full address, home telephone number, date of birth, and, below that information, the title of the contest subject you selected when you wrote your story. You may enter a story in one, two, or all three contest categories, but a separate Entry Form or Card must accompany each entry, and each entry must be mailed to Bantam in a separate envelope bearing sufficient postage. Completed Entry Forms or Cards, along with your typed story, should be sent to:

   > BANTAM BOOKS
   > LOVESWEPT WEDDING CONTEST
   > Department NT
   > 666 Fifth Avenue
   > New York, New York 10103

   All stories become the property of Bantam Books upon entry, and none will be returned. All stories entered must be original stories that are the sole and exclusive property of the entrant.

2. *First Prizes (3).* Three stories will be selected by the LOVESWEPT editors as winners in the LOVESWEPT WEDDING CONTEST, one story on each subject. The prize to be awarded to the author of the story selected as the First Prize winner of each subject-matter category will be the opportunity to meet with a LOVESWEPT editor to discuss the story idea of the winning entry, as well as publishing opportunities with LOVESWEPT. This meeting will occur at either the Romance Writers of America convention to be held in Chicago in July 1992 or at Bantam's offices in New York City. Any travel and accommodations necessary for the meeting are the responsibility of the contest winners and will not be provided by Bantam, but the winners will be able to select whether they would rather meet in Chicago or New York. If any First Prize winner is unable to travel in order to meet with the editor, that winner will have an opportunity to have the First Prize discussion via an extended telephone conversation with a LOVESWEPT editor. The First Prize winners will also be sent all six LOVESWEPT titles every month for a year (approximate retail value: $200.00).

   Second Prizes (3). One runner-up in each subject-matter category will be sent all six LOVESWEPT titles every month for six months (approximate retail value: $100.00).

3. All completed entries must be postmarked and received by Bantam no later than January 15, 1992. Entrants must be over the age of 21 on the date of entry. Bantam is not responsible for lost or misdirected or incomplete entries. The stories entered in the contest will be judged by Bantam's LOVESWEPT editors, and the winners will be selected on the basis of the originality, creativity, and

writing ability shown in the stories. All of Bantam's decisions are final and binding. Winners will be notified on or about May 1, 1992. Winners have 30 days from date of notice in which to accept their prize award, or an alternative winner will be chosen. If there are insufficient entries or if, in the judges' sole opinion, no entry is suitable or adequately meets any given subject as described above, Bantam reserves the right not to declare a winner for either or both of the prizes in any particular subject-matter category. There will be no prize substitutions allowed and no promise of publication is implied by winning the contest.

4. Each winner will be required to sign an Affidavit of Eligibility and Promotional Release supplied by Bantam. Entering the contest constitutes permission for use of the winner's name, address, biographical data, likeness, and contest story for publicity and promotional purposes, with no additional compensation.

5. The contest is open to residents in the U.S. and Canada, excluding the Province of Quebec, and is void where prohibited by law. All federal and local regulations apply. Employees of Bantam Books, Bantam Doubleday Dell Publishing Group, Inc., their subsidiaries and affiliates, and their immediate family members are ineligible to enter. Taxes, if any, are the responsibility of the winners.

6. For a list of winners, available after June 15, 1992, send a self-addressed stamped envelope to WINNERS LIST, LOVESWEPT WEDDING CONTEST, Department NT, 666 Fifth Avenue, New York, New York 10103.

OFFICIAL ENTRY FORM

BANTAM BOOKS
LOVESWEPT WEDDING CONTEST
Department NT
666 Fifth Avenue
New York, New York 10103

NAME _____

ADDRESS _____

CITY _____ STATE _____ ZIP _____

HOME TELEPHONE NUMBER _____

DATE OF BIRTH _____

CONTEST SUBJECT FOR THIS STORY IS: _____

_____

SIGNATURE CONSENTING TO ENTRY _____

_____

FANFARE
On Sale in January

LIGHTS ALONG THE SHORE
☐ (29331-1) $5.99/6.99 in Canada
by Diane Austell

Marin Gentry would become a woman to be reckoned with -- but a woman who must finally admit how she longs to be loved.
A completely involving and satisfying novel, and the debut of a major storyteller.

LAWLESS
☐ (29071-1) $4.99/5.99 in Canada
by Patricia Potter
author of RAINBOW

Willow Taylor held within her heart a love of the open frontier -- and a passion for a renegade gunman called Lobo -- the lone wolf.
Their hearts ran free in a land that was LAWLESS . . .

HIGHLAND REBEL
☐ (29836-5) $4.99/5.99 in Canada
by Stephanie Bartlett
author of HIGHLAND JADE

Catriona Galbraith was a proud Highland beauty consumed with the fight to save the lush rolling hills of her beloved home, the Isle of Skye. Ian MacLeod was the bold American sworn to win her love.